Stone of Destiny

LAURA HOWARD

Stone of Destiny
Book Two of *The Danaan Trilogy*

Copyright © 2014 by Laura Howard
Formatting by Self Publishing Editing Service
Publishing by Finding Bliss Publishing

ISBN: 978-0692207123

Dedication

For Kevin, Erin, Colleen, Ryan and Owen. You are my heart.

Pronunciation Guide

Liam {Lee-um}

Niamh {Neev}

Aoife {Ay-fuh}

Breanh {Bran}

Diarmuid {Der-mott}

Niall {Neal}

Bláithín {Blaw-heen}

Eithne {En-ya}

Aodhan {Ay-den}

Saoirse {Sare-shuh}

Deaghlan {Deck-lun}

Ciarán {Kee-run}

Maire {Mah-ree}

Tír na n'Óg {Tur-na-nog}

Bruidhean {Brood-ian}

Fháillan {Fah-lan}

Chapter One

"Aoife has escaped."

My jaw dropped at Liam's words. I'd known this already, but now the others knew that Aoife was no longer imprisoned in the fey globe. I kept quiet as I tried to gauge my father's reaction. He didn't sound frightened or nervous. He sounded tired. Like he'd been expecting this to happen for some time now.

I glanced at Aodhan who leaned against my SUV, arms folded across his massive chest. He didn't meet my eyes right away, but glowered off into the distance. When he eventually looked at me, his expression was carefully blank. I didn't need to be able to read body language to know how he felt about Aoife's escape. Aodhan despised all the Danaan. Like Liam, he was once a human living in Ireland. When a British soldier shot him and left him to die in 1600 Niamh, a Danaan princess brought him home with her to Tír na n'Óg.

A Danaan is what most people refer to as a member of the Fair Folk or, as much as I hate the term, a faerie. They look almost human but are so flawless that it gives them an ethereal appearance. That's where the similarities end. They don't have human feelings or consciences. They do what pleases them with no regard for who gets hurt along the way.

The ultimate example of their race stood in my personal space as my father spoke.

Deaghlan, king of the Danaans, was inhumanly beauti-ful. His black hair was long enough to touch the collar of his tight gray T-shirt. His face was the perfect combination of hard lines and smooth skin. But more than any of his features combined, his eyes were the most captivating. Bright blue and hypnotic. I'd been trapped in his gaze way more than I'd care to admit. Humans rarely resist the Danaans charm. And they delighted in toying with us.

Deaghlan studied my face. His dark eyebrows furrowed as he watched my reaction. Aoife was his daughter, although since Danaans are immortal he didn't look much older than me, twenty-five at most. A smirk lingered on his lips and I knew he was enjoying himself. Human concerns amused him. For the king of such a powerful race, I found it strange that everything was always a joke to him.

Liam cleared his throat and I cursed under my breath. Once again I had been completely mesmerized by Deaghlan. No matter how many times I told myself not to look into his eyes, I always fell into the same trap whenever he was near me — wide-eyed and staring like one of those vacant dolls in the toy store. Warmth burned in my chest, spreading quickly to my throat as I wrenched my gaze away.

When humans looked into Danaans' eyes, they became enraptured, turned into mindless slaves who would walk through fire just to be close to them. The Danaans didn't al-ways do it on purpose, but it probably came in handy when they were looking to score. And once a human had a physical relationship with a Danaan, all hope of regaining free will was gone. Since the Danaans didn't normally stick around, those humans were driven crazy, like addicts waiting for their next fix. One that would never come.

"Do you know where she is now?" I asked.

Liam frowned and paused before answering. "Not yet. We came straight here to check on your mother. She's okay, I take it?"

I looked up at my grandparents' house where I'd lived

my entire life. I hadn't met Liam until a few months ago when he showed up on our doorstep with his stories of Danaans and magic. My grandparents raised me because my mother was diagnosed with paranoid schizophrenia shortly after I was born.

I inhaled. "I just got home from orientation, but I *think* she's fine." Surely my grandparents would've called my cell if anything were wrong.

I started walking toward the house. "Wait here. I'll only be a second."

I climbed the wooden stairs that led onto the porch of the big farmhouse. Feeling all three pairs of eyes on my back, I reached for the handle of the screen door. When I swung it open, I jumped and stifled a yelp. My mother stood directly in front of me, staring over my shoulder to where Liam and the others waited.

"Mom," I said, running a hand over my mouth. "What are you doing? Where's Gram?"

My mother's green eyes flitted from Liam to me and back again, but she didn't answer.

What the doctor's believed was schizophrenia was actually the supernatural addiction my mother held for my father. Before they met, my mom was normal and healthy. She went to college and traveled to Ireland during her final semester to study music at Trinity. They met at the Music in the Street Festival. They fell in love almost immediately despite my father's complicated relationship with Deaghlan's other daughter, Aoife.

Aoife didn't just get jealous when she found out my father was in love with someone else. Oh no, that would be what a human would do. Aoife cast a magical enchantment, called a *geis*, on my father. The *geis* prevented my father from touching my mother. My mother would be driven mad without his touch, and eventually die of a broken heart. Not only that, but Aoife forbade my father from leaving Tír na n'Óg.

Just months ago Aoife's sister Niamh had helped my father escape by trapping Aoife in a magical glass prison called a fey globe. He came to America to find my mother and met me instead. He didn't know anything about me, so he was pretty surprised his daughter answered the door when he came calling. In his defense, time passed in a completely different way in Tír na n'Óg. Each year there was the equivalent of about twenty years here.

Needless to say, I wasn't excited to welcome him into our lives. I hadn't even told my grandparents about him yet. I had many reasons for that, but the most important was that since my father spent so much time in their realm, he became mostly Danaan himself. He became immortal, and like the fully grown Danaan, he looked about twenty-five.

I hadn't figured out a way to explain that my father looked like he could be my brother. Because of her relationship with my father, my mom hadn't aged much either. But her behavior was so unpredictable and sometimes frightening that people don't ask about how she looks.

I pulled the heavy wooden door shut behind me and locked the deadbolt. I hoped having Liam out of sight might keep my mother from breaking down.

"Gram," I called as I walked past the staircase and down the hallway to the kitchen in the back of the house.

"Hello sweetheart," my grandmother said, looking up at me with a smile. She sat at the kitchen table with a stack of bills and her checkbook.

"How was orientation?" Gram asked.

"It was fine," I said. "How's Mom?" The sound of fiddle music floated out to the kitchen from the den.

Gram straightened her pile of papers and looked at me over her reading glasses. "She seems fine today. Why do you ask?"

I grabbed a plum out of the fruit bowl and shrugged. "Oh, no reason. I was just thinking about her on my ride home."

"All right then," Gram said, focusing back on her bills.

"I'm going to take a walk. I won't be gone long," I called over my shoulder as I hurried past the den and headed back out to the driveway.

I froze on the bottom step when I realized what I'd forgotten.

Before Liam had shared the news about Aoife, I'd stopped next door at my cousin Nicole's house. I'd walked into the pool area to find not only Nicole and her boyfriend Jeff, but Jeff's brother, Ethan, and some blonde girl I didn't know. I'd just decided to admit my feelings to Ethan after years of pushing him away. But the way the blonde was attached to Ethan stopped me cold. I'd fled feeling like I'd been punched in the gut.

Ethan had followed me out of the pool area and that's when I came face to face with the Danaans in my driveway. Sometime between Liam's news and me checking on my mother, Ethan had disappeared.

Hurt swelled just beneath my skin as I headed down the walk toward my car. Even though we weren't together, every time I saw Ethan with another girl it felt like the world stopped spinning.

He could have been yours. My subconscious taunted me. Ethan told me he wanted me many times over the years. And I'd come so close to admitting my feelings to him. But things were so complicated before that I didn't want to drag him into the rabbit hole with me. And now…

"Allison," Liam said.

I frowned and followed the sound of his voice to the sidewalk where he waited with Aodhan and Deaghlan.

"I haven't had a chance to show you the house," Liam said, motioning for me to follow him.

Shortly after I met my father, he bought the vacant lot beside my grandparents' house. It was creepy at first, but it was convenient to have a place to speak in private about Aoife.

The house was built by Magliaro Construction, Ethan's father's company. It was one level and appeared small from outside, but the vaulted ceilings and shiny hardwoods inside made it seem much bigger.

The house was pretty empty. The only furniture was a large oak table in the dining room. Aodhan marched right into the kitchen that joined the dining room. His eyes scanned every surface, like he was expecting the boogeyman to jump out from behind the door. Satisfied for the moment, he leaned back against the countertop and folded his arms.

I sat at the table, trying to ignore how closely Deaghlan followed me. He slid into the chair next to mine and stretched out his legs. From the corner of my eye I could see he was watching me, but I wouldn't look directly at him.

"The most important thing is that Elizabeth is safe for the moment," Liam said. He leaned on the back of a chair and met my eyes.

I nodded, but no matter how much I wanted to tell them I'd known all along Aoife wasn't still trapped in the fey globe, it was impossible to say it out loud. Aoife told me I couldn't t say a word about it to anyone. She'd used mind control before she disappeared in Tír na n'Óg and I *literally* couldn't speak of it.

"We need to figure out who set her free," Aodhan said, clearly agitated. His Irish brogue became thicker and harder to understand when he was alarmed.

Deaghlan laughed beside me. "That isn't hard to figure out, is it?"

The three of us turned to Deaghlan expectantly. He shook his head and chuckled. "My bet is on Saoirse. I would've done it myself if I had a chance."

Saoirse was the queen of Tír na n'Óg, Aoife and Niamh's mother. In Danaan society, the queen was the most powerful member of the race. But when I'd met her, she'd seemed very interested in restoring order after all the chaos Aoife created.

"No, it couldn't be." Liam swallowed and rubbed his palms over his face. "Saoirse knows what Aoife has done. She wouldn't let her out of her sight."

Deaghlan wrapped the end of my ponytail around his finger and laughed when I cringed. "We'll see."

Aodhan's eyes narrowed and the muscles in his jaw tensed. I could tell he wanted to say more, but he kept quiet. Once Deaghlan was gone I hoped to hear what he really thought. Since Aodhan came back to the human realm in 1888, he spent his days as a self-imposed vigilante. Every time one of the Danaans stepped out of line, Aodhan knew about it and put an end to it immediately. Danaans were sometimes to blame for stories on the news, usually just pranks or cases of unexplained amnesia.

But recently in Canada, a group of Danaans started siphoning human blood for some forbidden magic that Aoife was involved in. Liam told me this ancient magic was forbidden by Saoirse because it made the Danaans do terrible things, such as draining their victims and tossing their bodies in the gutter. Liam and I found Aodhan by going to Thunder Bay in Ontario where the reports of a blood-thirsty serial killer were all over the news. I'd gotten a glimpse of what this forbidden magic did to the Danaans. The one I saw looked like a strung-out heroin addict.

"Well, if there isn't anything we can do for now, I have to get ready for work," I said, moving away from the table and Deaghlan's maddening faerie mojo.

Chapter 2

I've worked three or four days a week at my grandfather's hardware store since I was a junior in high school. O'Malley's Hardware is only about a mile and a half from our house in Stoneville. I left the house about ten minutes before the start of my shift at three.

As I rolled up to the stop sign at the end of our road, my little SUV started making an odd thumping noise. I glanced at the dashboard, but none of the warning lights were on. Once I was sure there were no oncoming cars, I turned onto Main Street. The thump grew louder as I sped up and I figured I better pull over at Murphy's Convenience Store.

It was coming from the front passenger side and sure enough when I walked around the hood, my tire was flat. I cursed internally at not renewing my membership to AAA this year. I never had to change a tire and wasn't sure how.

I pulled out my phone to call my grandfather just as the door to Murphy's jangled behind me.

Glancing over my shoulder, I recognized a slightly familiar blonde holding the door for someone behind her. Ethan walked out and stopped when he saw me.

All the blood drained from my face at seeing them together again. I wasn't sure what to say, so I focused on my flat tire, hoping they'd be on their way.

"Allison," Ethan said, his voice apathetic.

I fought to make my expression equally cool before turning to face him "Oh, hey Ethan."

"Having a little trouble?" he asked, nodding at my tire.

"Yeah, you could say that."

Ethan took two steps toward me and froze. I looked up at his face and he seemed confused for a second. Then his expression shifted back and he laughed. It wasn't like he was laughing at a joke, not a playful laugh. It was cruel, like he was laughing *at* me. My heart turned to icy lead in my chest and I turned away.

"Well, *that sucks*," he said as he dropped his arm over the blonde's shoulder and walked toward the gas pumps where his truck was parked.

I chewed my lip as I stared at the tire. Ethan's behavior was so at odds with the guy I knew. I guess I didn't deserve his help after the way I'd ended things. I mean, we'd only hung out a few times and then there were those kisses. I'd told him none of it meant anything to me, but only because I didn't want him mixed up in any of the strange stuff that had been happening to me. But for him to walk away laughing at me was just plain mean.

I needed to figure out how to fix this, no matter how humiliated I felt. I'd seen plenty of tire changes in my life. It was time I took care of myself for once.

I popped open the rear door and pulled out my jack and lug wrench. After laying them out next to my flat, I discreetly searched for directions to change a tire on my phone. I found a quick tutorial online and followed each step. Unscrewing the bolts was the hardest part, but I stomped on the wrench and managed to get them off. It probably took three times as long as it should have, but when I tightened the final bolt on the spare and hauled the flat into the back, I dusted off my hands and smiled in satisfaction.

I arrived at work almost forty-five minutes late. Even still, my grandfather insisted on taking my car to have a new tire installed. I relented, knowing I wouldn't win this argument. My only concession was that he had to let me pay him back.

After Pop left, I spent the entire evening placing the orders he'd left for me. He always said he had no interest in learning how to do it over the computer, so I took it on since it was so much faster than trying to do it all over the phone. Between that and the few customers that came in, I replayed the scene with Ethan over and over in my mind.

Tonight called for an Extra Large Peanut Butter Cup Sundae and a *Persuasion* reread.

I'm walking in a grassy field at night, searching for something, and somehow I know it's important. Someone tugs on my hand, and I turn to see Ethan smile at me. His face is pinched in worry, but I can tell he's trying to reassure me.

The air is filled with the sound of low chanting. The strange rhythmic singing causes goose bumps to cover my arms. Up ahead flames and smoke swirl toward the inky sky.

I woke up to fingers of pale light spreading across the ceiling of my bedroom. The air was already thick with humidity and if I didn't force myself out of bed now, I would never get a run in.

I changed out of my pajamas and put on jogging shorts and a light tank top. I stretched my arms above my head, the chanting from my dream still vibrating deep in my bones.

For most of my life I've had dreams that felt like they were somehow *more* than just dreams. I learned from Saoirse, the queen, that there's a small amount of magic in my blood. She said they're called *True Dreams,* which was a diluted version of The Sight. Some Danaans have visions of the future or the past, but when a human has the ability it's called The Sight. The queen was a strong seer, but with the gift bestowed on all Danaan queens, Danu's Basin, a magical well in Tír na n'Óg, she sees every possible way the future can play out at will.

The house was quiet as I slipped out the front door. Our road was on the outskirts of Stoneville, so even in the middle of the day we didn't see much traffic. I cherished my morning run almost more than a hot fudge sundae with extra whipped cream. Something about the wind in my face and the pumping of my heart recharged me. I could make sense of almost any situation as long as my feet were carrying me forward and I had the peace of the open road.

The memory of Aoife's icy blue eyes was in the forefront of my thoughts. I wondered why she was so obsessed with my father. I felt a little bit guilty for having that thought, but what was it about Liam that made her so ruthless? The truth was I really didn't know anything about Aoife or Niamh, or any of the Danaans really. To keep my mother safe, I needed to learn more about what I was dealing with. From what I knew, we weren't in any immediate danger from Aoife. Aodhan wouldn't be so calm if that were the case.

As I jogged past my father's house on my way back home, a familiar blonde leaned casually on Liam's front fence post. Niamh stood gracefully, and I stopped when she met my eyes.

Good morning, Allison.

Niamh was a telepath. She could read my thoughts, and project her thoughts into my mind. It unnerved me and she knew it.

She actually looked apologetic, having picked my discomfort out of my thoughts. "I sometimes forget how that bothers you."

"No big deal. What's up?" I said as I bent down to stretch.

"I wanted to speak with you, but Liam stopped me. He told me your morning run is important to you."

I laughed to myself a little imagining Liam telling her what to do. Niamh was one of the good guys, as far as Danaans went. Even though she had technically kidnapped my mother and hidden her in Tír na n'Óg, it was for her own protection. Saoirse had foreseen that Aoife's adviser, Breanh, was planning to kidnap my mother. He would hold her hostage until Niamh and Liam let Aoife go.

Breanh was a telepath too, and if Niamh had told me that she was hiding my mother, Breanh would have read it in my thoughts. According to Saoirse, Breanh would have found another way to bargain for Aoife's release. In the end he did find another way, by kidnapping Ethan. But at least Niamh's intentions were good.

I raised my eyebrows at Niamh who was staring at me. She tossed her golden hair over one shoulder and looked up at the sky before she spoke.

"We haven't had the chance to speak since we came back, have we?" She glanced back at Liam's house with what I thought might be a nervous expression. She turned back to me and started leading me toward my grandparents' house. "I thought you might tell me a bit more about what happened with Breanh."

I frowned as I walked with her. I'd told this story several times and most of those times Niamh had been there.

"You're right, of course," she said in response to my thoughts. "But I can't help feeling you're having a hard time talking about it with all of those men. I understand that. They *are* intimidating aren't they?"

Niamh was one of the most self-possessed people I'd ever met. The idea of her being intimidated by anyone was bizarre. The only time I'd seen her control waver was when Aodhan was around. Their history was complicated. That probably explained why she was sitting on my front steps rather than Liam's. Aodhan had been staying at Liam's since we'd come back from Tír na n'Óg.

"There's not much more to tell," I said. No matter how

much I *wanted* to tell her the truth about Aoife, I couldn't. As soon as I thought it, Niamh's eyes widened just the tiniest bit, but it was enough to let me know she heard it in my mind.

I closed my eyes and the memory of Aoife killing Breanh played out in my mind. Aoife used mind control to keep me quiet, but could Niamh really see this? I never realized there was a loophole.

She nodded and cocked her head to the side, thinking. "Aoife wasn't there when Aodhan found you. She must have snuck back through the portal. She didn't say where she planned to go?"

I shook my head. One minute Aoife was standing in front of me and the next, I heard the sound of Aodhan's boots from the corridor. I looked to see who was coming and when I turned back, Aoife was gone.

"Where does her portal lead to?" I asked.

"The only place I know for certain is an old castle outside of Dublin." Niamh tapped her finger on her lower lip for a second and turned to me. "I believe she created a portal somewhere near Thunder Bay. That's where all the trouble from her guards has been. My mother will know the exact location."

I stretched my legs out in front of me on the steps. "Aodhan mentioned more reports of murders in Thunder Bay, even after your guards killed Aengus, the one who stabbed Liam."

Niamh sighed. "I hope if my sister *is* there she'll put an end to that. If only because she doesn't want the unnecessary attention."

"Why does Aoife use magic that's supposed to be forbidden, anyway?" I asked.

It was several seconds before Niamh answered. "Aoife hasn't always been so troublesome," she said. "I was nearly full-grown when she was born. She followed me around, always curious about what I was doing. When she was just a halfling, which is about the same as a ten year old human child, I brought Aodhan to Tír na n'Óg."

I couldn't believe Niamh was being so open with me, so I kept quiet hoping she'd continue. She chuckled quietly, hearing that thought.

"Aoife was fond of Aodhan. At that time, he adored her as well. It was impossible not to be enraptured by her big blue eyes and thick black curls. As she got older, Aoife grew jealous of the relationship between Aodhan and me. Few Danaans experience love." Niamh paused and looked down at her hands before meeting my gaze. "I consider myself lucky to have been loved by Aodhan once. I know you've wondered about that..."

I nodded. I *had* wondered about the relationship between Niamh and Aodhan, only knowing that Niamh had rescued Aodhan after he'd been shot by English soldiers in 1602.

"When Aoife met your father, she thought she'd found a love of her own, similar to Aodhan and me. Unfortunately for her, Liam was merely enthralled by her. When that wore off he wasn't in love with her at all. She still hasn't accepted that and probably never will. She tries to rationalize what she's done to him by believing his love for your mother is a passing fancy. When you have all the time in the world, as we do, a human life span seems rather insignificant." She smiled vaguely.

"So she thinks he'll get over it and come back to her someday?"

"Yes. But we are a vain people, I admit. Aoife doesn't understand why Liam would love your mother when he could have someone such as herself."

A breeze ruffled the hair that came loose from my ponytail. When I looked up, Deaghlan was right beside me, resting his arm on the porch railing.

"So jealous of a human—I'll never understand," he said. But when he looked down at me his eyes smoldered. I laced my fingers together around my knees to keep from doing something I'd probably regret.

"Good morning, Father." Niamh shot me an amused look.

"Speaking of humans, Allison, how have things been going between you and your human friend? What was his name—Ethan?"

I glared up at him, making the mistake of meeting his dazzling blue eyes. He wore a snug light blue V-neck shirt that brought the color out even more. I blinked and shook my head, trying to remember what his question was.

"Ethan? He's been…busy. I guess. I haven't seen much of him."

"Hmm, too bad. He seemed like such an *interesting* boy." Deaghlan's eyebrow quirked up. He seemed pleased with himself.

Don't let him get to you. He's just trying to get a reaction.

Taking Niamh's silent warning, I looked down at the ground, pressing my lips together.

"You know, Niamh, you really should be spending more time learning about Allison's abilities," Deaghlan said, his eyes eager with curiosity. "Her mind shields are practically non-existent. Rather than worrying about what Aoife is doing, don't you think you'd be better off teaching Allison how to see through glamour?"

"I'm still here, you know." I said, annoyed.

"I was actually planning on going home." Niamh said. "I'd like to speak with Mother about a few things."

Deaghlan waved his hand. He obviously didn't think anything Aoife did was wrong. To him we were just like Niamh said, *insignificant.*

I'd had my share of Deaghlan for the morning and excused myself, practically tasting the incredulity coming off of Deaghlan as the screen door shut behind me.

I walked down the hall, past the stairs into the living room. My grandparents and mother sat at the little round table that separated the living room from the kitchen. Like most mornings, my grandfather was eating a bowl of cereal while talking with my grandmother. I grabbed a cup of coffee before joining them.

I took the first sip before I realized what my mother was doing. She had a mostly blank piece of sheet music in front of her. Her brow was furrowed as she filled in notes on the page. Without saying anything I met my grandmother's gaze and widened my eyes, wondering if she was seeing what I was seeing. Her answering smile told me she was.

My mother was a musical prodigy from the time she was old enough to hold a fiddle under her chin. She'd taken private lessons and traveled across the country to perform with a handful of other talented young musicians called the Fiddle Kids. She not only had talent, but a magical stage presence that drove the audiences wild. My grandparents had some old videos of my mom at eleven, playing while my Aunt Jessie, age nine, danced a traditional Irish jig. They made it look as easy as breathing, which I'd learned through my own lessons was certainly not the case.

I never saw my mother write music before. She wrote a few pieces in college, but her days of composing ended after she met my father. To see her even attempting to put notes together was incredible. So much happened since I'd met my father and I couldn't help wondering what had changed with her. Was she better when he was near? Could it be that time was erasing the thrall she was under?

A buzz and a series of beeps announced a new message on my phone, so I got up and grabbed it off the side table by the hall.

The text was from my cousin, Nicole.

I'm coming over. You better be awake!

I put my phone back as the front door banged open. Nicole sashayed to where I stood, her eyes bright. She squeezed my upper arms and flounced toward the table where my family still sat.

"I have some news," she said as she kissed the top of my mother's head. My grandparents chuckled at her as she breezed toward the coffee.

"Well, don't let us stop you from having your coffee," Pop said, his eyes twinkling with mirth.

I sat back down and watched Nicole heap sugar into her cup

Without turning she said, "Jeff took me to Boston last night, as you all know." She spun around and leaned back on the counter as she took a long sip of coffee. She drew out the moment before placing the cup on the counter. "He asked me to marry him." Her voice was nearly a shriek as she held out her bejeweled finger in front of her.

"Oh my word, sweetheart," Gram said and stood to wrap her arms around Nicole. "Congratulations."

"Congrats, Nic," I said with a wink. "I was wondering what he was waiting for."

"Well, it's not in my nature to make you wait, is it?" Nicole asked me sweetly. A little too sweetly. "Allison, will you please be my maid of honor?"

Everyone laughed as she came over and took my hands in hers. The sheer joy on her face was enough to keep me from ruining her moment with sarcasm.

"Of course I will," I said and pulled my hands out of hers so I could hug her. "I'm so happy for you, both of you."

When she met my eyes, I could see tears welling in hers and I looked away. Seeing someone else cry always made tears burn the back of my own eyes.

"Did you talk about a date yet, small fry?" Pop asked before taking the last bite of his cereal.

Nicole straightened and put her hand on her chin. "Well, I've always wanted a traditional June wedding. That will give us nine months, plenty of time to plan, right Al?"

I groaned in mock horror. "Not nearly enough," I muttered, but I grinned at her.

Chapter Three

The semester didn't begin for another four days, so I went into work at the store for noon. I said hello to my grandfather's other employee, Lenny, and let him know I was there to take over.

As I reached under the counter to grab my O'Malley Hardware apron, the hairs on the back of my neck stood up. I glanced up to see if anyone was around, then froze when I saw Ethan standing at the back of the store by the ladders. His eyes were locked on mine, an unruly dark curl fell over his forehead as he tilted his head. I waved and swallowed hard. While tying the apron around my waist, I still felt his eyes on me.

I told Lenny goodbye and got to work unpacking a box of key-rings for the counter display. I chanced a look and Ethan was two aisles back, trailing his fingers over a stack of clotheslines, watching me. A rush of heat ignited my skin. He smirked and walked slowly to the register.

"Allison," Ethan said, a mischievous grin forming on his lips. It had been so long since I'd seen him smile, my heart skipped a beat.

I raised my eyebrows, remembering the cruel way he laughed at me just yesterday when I had a flat tire. "Hey Ethan, how are things?" I tried to keep my tone light, wincing when my voice came out shaky.

"Not too bad," he said. The way he was looking at me

was doing funny things to my pulse and I wiped my clammy hands on my pants before hanging the keyrings on the little metal rack. The more he stared, the harder it was to keep my breathing under control. Why was he doing this to me?

He started laughing, but it sounded all wrong. My eyes flew up to meet his and in a flash, his body rippled and transformed into the body of Deaghlan. My breath caught and I grabbed the countertop with one hand as the other flew up to my mouth.

"Deaghlan, what the hell?" I said. My brain was still trying to catch up with the fact that Deaghlan stood in front of me, staring at me with an unsettling grin.

His expression remained amused as he ran one long finger over the counter. "Sorry to disappoint, Allison. Tell me, what do you find so irresistible about Ethan?"

I blinked at him and shook my head. Deaghlan, a king, a man more powerful than I could probably fathom, was playing tricks on me like we were in second grade.

"You're crazy," I said, peeling my eyes away from his impossibly high cheekbones and blazing blue eyes. I would be lost forever if I allowed myself to fall under Deaghlan's thrall. The only explanation I could imagine for his relentless attention was that I provided him with a diversion from the boredom that came with immortality.

"Undoubtedly," he agreed.

"I was planning on seducing you in that guise." He shrugged, his eyes roaming around the store. "But the amount of iron in this building is so distracting. How can you stand it?"

Iron didn't exist in Tír na n'Óg. Close proximity in the human realm weakened them unless they used a bit of elemental magic, even though it was supposedly forbidden. They wore arm bands and necklaces made from a mineral from their world called fháillan, carved with runes, to ward off the effects of iron.

I turned to straighten the workspace that held the credit

card machines. With my back to him I said, "I'm *just a human* Deaghlan, remember? Iron doesn't bother me."

"No, you've a fair amount of magic in your blood Allison. Your ancestors, not just Liam, have had dalliances with the Danaan, I think. You're much too attractive to be fully human. Not only that but you're incredibly intriguing."

I turned my head and spoke over my shoulder. "I'm *not* your shiny new toy."

Before I could regret speaking so harshly, his body was pressed against my side, his cool breath tickling my ear. "Aren't you, though?"

And then he was gone, the only sound the jingling of the door bells.

I finished the rest of my shift without incident. I was able to complete several mundane tasks to keep my mind off the helpless feeling Deaghlan had left me with.

Once I'd closed the store for the night, I headed to Liam's house. When I pulled into his long, unpaved driveway and parked, the garage door was open. Aodhan sat in front of a bench with his back to me. He was working rigorously on something, his shoulders hunched in concentration.

When I pulled up the stool beside him he placed a small tin flute on the workbench. He treated it with the same care and reverence as he did a knife or sword.

"Good evening, Allison."

I smiled, the image of him playing the little instrument at odds with his hulking figure. Aodhan was the son of an Irish chieftain. During our time together he'd told me a few stories of the battles he'd fought and also his love for music.

"Is Liam inside?" I asked, nodding toward the door that led into the house.

He sighed and ran a hand over his buzzed head. "Yes. Diarmuid and Eithne are here."

"Diarmuid's here? What's going on?" Diarmuid was Niamh's adviser, like a second in command. He was keeping watch over the portal to Tír na n'Óg in Wheelwright while she was away. He was bonded to Eithne, a healer and former handmaiden of Aoife. I'd met them a couple times when my mother was missing. They were the only Danaan's I knew who were bonded for love.

"Nothing much," Aodhan said, eyeing the door again. "Diarmuid is giving Niamh an update from the guards in Thunder Bay."

"All right," I said, trying to think how I should ask my next question. "Something happened tonight. I need to tell you about it, but I don't want anyone else to hear."

He frowned, but gestured for me to follow as he led me out of the garage and down toward the street.

"So, while I was working, Deaghlan came into the store."

He stopped walking and raised his brows.

"You know how he is around me." I laughed nervously. "Well, this was worse than usual. He was glamoured to look like Ethan."

Aodhan pressed his lips together and put both of his hands on his head before he began walking again.

"But he let his glamour down, let you know it was really him while he was there?"

"Yeah. I guess I should've known it wasn't Ethan, since he was smiling at me."

He glanced at me, a deep furrow in his brow. "I don't know how to make him understand there are things going on here more important than his amusement."

"The thing that's really bothering me is that I *thought* I could see through glamour. Couldn't Aoife be hiding in plain sight, glamoured to look like my grandmother or something?"

He stared straight ahead as he marched up the sidewalk. It was hard to see his face in the dark, although anger poured off of him in waves.

"I know this isn't what you want to hear," he said, his

voice low. "But, you can't trust anyone. You're right, Aoife could be anywhere. You'll see glamour if you're looking for it. But you always have to pay attention. Look twice at your friends. Don't take anything for granted."

"Allison?"

I spun around to find Liam walking behind us, concern etched on his forehead.

"I saw your vehicle in the drive. Is everything all right?"

"Um, yeah. I just needed someone to talk to in private. But I want you to know, too." I told him about Deaghlan.

"Aodhan's right," he said, looking down at the street as he passed a hand through his hair. "When I was catching up to you I heard him say you mustn't trust anyone. Not for now, at least."

Chapter Four

An uneasy routine formed in my life over the next week. School began again, I ran just about every morning, and worked a few times at the store. I saw Liam nearly every day, but we didn't make any plans to find Aoife. He told me only one of Niamh's guards was back in place in Thunder Bay watching for Aoife. We were pretty much stuck doing nothing until we knew what we were dealing with.

Friday afternoon I came home from classes and grabbed the mail. Inside was an invitation to the engagement party for Nicole and Jeff the following weekend. Operation Bride was on. Being the quintessential Italian family, the Magliaros were having the party at Angela's Ristorante, which belonged to Jeff and Ethan's Uncle Al.

When I brought the mail into the house, the rich scent of barbecue sauce hit me. My grandmother made the most delicious pulled pork in the entire world.

"I smell heaven," I said as I dropped the stack of mail onto the sideboard. Gram smiled over her shoulder from where she washed her hands at the sink.

"There's my Allie-girl. How was school?"

"Not too bad," I said as I followed the sweet smell into the kitchen. Gram had her big crockpot out, filled to the brim with pork, which meant we were having company.

"Are we having a party?" I asked, breathing deep.

"Aunt Jessie and Uncle David and Nicole and Jeff will

be eating with us. Kind of a mini-engagement party."

It smells great," I said, kissing Gram on the cheek before retreating to my room to start my homework.

It seemed like I had just sat down when I heard the door close and muffled voices came from the front hall. I finished up my Statistics homework and put my books away in my backpack.

I started down the stairs just in time to hear Jeff and Ethan's mother, Joanne, talking to Gram.

"Thank you for inviting us, dinner smells wonderful. I wish you would have let me bring something."

Gram made a sound of exasperation and I could see her waving her hand at Joanne. "I'm just glad you could come last minute. Elizabeth will be so glad to see you."

Not only was Ethan's brother engaged to my cousin, but his mother was also my mother's lifelong best friend. In Stoneville everyone knew everyone.

Joanne saw me over my grandmother's shoulder and her face lit up. After she hugged me, she held me by the tops of my arms and met my eyes. "How are you, sweetie?"

"I'm doing great, keeping busy," I said, eyes roaming into the living room to see who else was here.

"He's not here," Joanne whispered in my ear. "He wouldn't tell me why, just that he couldn't come tonight."

I pulled back my shoulders and plastered on a smile. Trying not to sound too disappointed, I made small talk as we entered the living room. My grandparents and aunt and uncle all listened as Nicole told the story of Jeff proposing. Again. Jeff sat on the couch next to my mother, rolling his eyes and pointing his thumb at Nicole affectionately when he saw me.

After everyone was done eating, I jumped up and hurried into the kitchen to start on the dishes.

As I filled the sink with soapy water, Nicole came in and leaned against the counter next to me. I smiled half-heartedly without meeting her eyes.

"Have you been avoiding me?" She asked, reaching in front of me to shut off the water.

"Of course not. I don't know why you would even say that." But I still couldn't look at her.

"Whatever is going on between you and Ethan, don't let it come between us." She sighed. "He won't talk to me or even Jeff about it. You don't have to tell me what happened, but don't shut me out, okay?"

I gripped the edge of the counter and finally met her gaze. Her eyes were so sad my heart sank.

"I'm sorry," I whispered, touching her arm. She nodded, and her lower lip trembled a little.

"I didn't mean to hurt you. It's just hard to be around Ethan right now. But it's even harder seeing that he's not here and thinking it's because of me."

Nicole sniffed and leaned her head on my shoulder. "I'm sorry this is hard for you. I really miss you."

"I miss you too," I said. It was true. Nicole had been the only friend I'd ever really had. She'd always tried to include me in her plans, even when we were little girls, but I'd always been happier when it was just me and her.

"Are you coming to the engagement party?" she asked.

I cringed inside, but kept my voice light as I ruffled her blonde hair. "I wouldn't miss it for anything."

The school bus pulls up in front of the house. Three little girls pile out of the open doors. The first one, the one with a blonde bob, is Nicole. She is pulling on a taller girl's hand. The tall girl, Tina Donnelly, looks over her shoulder at the last girl and smiles, her two front teeth missing. The third girl with the light brown braids is me. I return her smile, but look away shyly. Aunt Jessie is sitting on my front porch with my mom, waiting for us. They look so much alike, except

Aunt Jessie is smiling and waving at us and my mother is staring at her hands in her lap.

I bite my lip and hesitate at the bottom of the stairs. This is the first time I've had a friend from school over. Nicole is so excited to have another girl to play tea party with and I don't want to ruin this for her because I'm nervous.

They follow me up to my bedroom where I proudly show them my white table and chairs with a perfectly displayed rose tea set.

We play and laugh and I become more comfortable with Tina. She's so nice and she really likes my toys.

Nicole announces that we need to get snacks for our tea party and I follow them down to the kitchen, caught up in the flurry of little girl giggles.

Aunt Jessie sits next to my mother on the couch and when we come bustling into the kitchen, my mother's eyes dart over to where the three of us stand. She jumps up off the couch and starts rubbing her hands over her face and shaking her head. I freeze when she begins mumbling about a castle and Liam and needing to get inside the door. Most of what she says doesn't make sense at all. I look over at Tina, her eyes wide and chewing her bottom lip.

It wasn't even light out when I woke up. I'd tossed and turned, remembering the first and last playdate I'd ever had. Aunt Jessie had sent us back up to my room so she could calm my mother down. Tina wouldn't talk to me or Nicole, she just kept saying she wanted to go home.

The kids in school all looked at me funny after that, she must have told the story of my crazy mother to the entire class.

I needed something to take my mind off the dream, and the mound of laundry I'd been avoiding finally summoned me.

I made a quick trip to the bathroom and as I washed my hands I looked at myself in the mirror. Despite how different my life had become, my reflection hadn't changed much in the past couple months. Pale skin, blue eyes almost too big for my face. My light brown hair was a little longer. Funny that Nicole hadn't complained about that, since she was my hairdresser. Admittedly she had other things on her mind. Normal, human things like getting married and what to have for dinner. I fought to contain my anger over my own fate.

I thought back to the times when, even as a little girl I stood in front of the same mirror wondering what was so different about me. Why wasn't I like all the other kids at school?

Before she completely succumbed to madness, my mother would sometimes stand behind me and run a comb through my hair. I'd watch her face in the mirror as she hummed tunes to me. Her eyes were an extraordinary shade of green, her hair a pale gold. I wished so many times that I looked like her, the way Nicole did. I sometimes wondered if Nicole was really her daughter and I was adopted.

I was about eight years old when I found the old photo booth shots of my parents together before I was born. That's when I discovered that I looked just like my father, which even now caused a bittersweet feeling in my chest. Knowing where you come from might not be essential, but it can change the way you see yourself. Knowing that my father loved my mother somehow made me feel like I was part of something I'd been missing. Little did I know that what I was part of was a life that felt more like a fairytale to me with each day.

Allison?

Niamh's thoughts reached in to my mind, and I shook my head to clear it.

If you're not busy, I thought we could work on glamour in Liam's yard.

I looked at my reflection one last time before heading down the stairs to meet Niamh next door. The rising sun cast a warm glow over the backyard. I walked through the little path in the wooded area between my house and Liam's.

Niamh sat on a large boulder wearing something I never thought I'd see her in — jeans and a T-shirt with flip-flops. She normally dressed in pencil skirts and pant suits straight out of a Neiman Marcus catalog. The change made her seem less intimidating, she could almost pass for human.

"Good morning," Niamh said in her usual self-assured manner.

"Morning," I said, lowering myself onto the boulder beside her.

"I hear my father has been giving you a hard time," she said, a glimmer of amusement in her eyes.

I huffed. "You could say that." If giving me a hard time translated to reveling in making me squirm at every opportunity.

Niamh smiled and I knew she heard it all. "This is what happens when my mother is focused on something. He gets bored."

"What's your mother so focused on?" I asked.

She stood up. "Mainly Aoife. And you."

A surprised laugh escaped my lips. "Why me?"

"We can talk about that later," she said, gesturing for me to get up. "Right now I want to show you how to see through glamour, while there's nobody around."

I got up and blew out a slow breath. My hands hung limply at my sides, not sure what I was supposed to do.

"Just watch me for a minute. You don't have to do anything yet."

Faster than a thought she appeared just a foot in front of me. Her clear blue eyes met mine and like a snake shedding its skin, she disappeared.

People can't see me if I don't want them to. I've basically compelled you not to see me. But you have The Sight, so you just have to look harder.

My father had taught me to see through glamour. I looked away from where I knew she stood and attempted to see her out of the corner of my eye. A silver sheen shaped like her body came into view. I looked straight at her outline until she came back into focus. Most humans couldn't do that.

"I can tell the instant you see me, not only because I hear your thoughts, but because your eyes naturally meet mine."

I nodded and shifted my weight.

"Let's try something else, so you can get an idea of what's possible."

Before she finished speaking, her form melted into Nicole. I blinked. It was eerie that nothing gave her away. Her posture was a little bit sassy, just like my cousin's.

"I don't actually look any different, it's all in how you perceive me," Niamh said in Nicole's voice. "I don't sound any different either."

"That's amazing," I said, tucking my hair back. "But, what would someone else see?"

"Glamour has a wide range. It's not like altering the memory of a single person. I send out a broad compulsion that affects everyone within about a half-mile radius, give or take."

My eyes widened in surprise. "Do you think I could do that?"

Niamh shook her head. "I don't. We can test your strength, but I would bet the most you could do is compel someone enough to distract them or get their attention."

"Okay," I said. And that was totally fine with me. Even that ability freaked me out. Knowing I wasn't able to perform some kind of Jedi mind tricks was actually comforting.

"Focus on staying alert and watching for glamour. Always look beyond what you see. Once you form the habit, it will come naturally."

"How?" I asked.

Niamh rubbed her hands together. "Here's what we'll do. I want you to close your eyes and count to five. When you open them I'll be invisible to you. Find me."

"Are you serious?"

She quirked an eyebrow up. "Very serious. This will be the most difficult for you, so it's the best place to start."

I closed my eyes and began counting. I reopened them and roamed around Liam's yard trying to catch a glimpse of Niamh's outline. There was no grass. It was still just a rectangle of packed dirt right up to the tree line.

You'll never see me if you're looking straight ahead.

I groaned at her voice in my head, but scanned my peripheral vision. After a few more minutes I almost gave up. I walked back to the boulder we'd been sitting on and a crow's loud caw had me nearly jumping out of my skin. That's when I saw the faint outline of Niamh sitting on the boulder, exactly as I'd first found her.

"Very clever," I said as her image came back into focus.

A wry grin lit up Niamh's face. She stood gracefully and like an old-fashioned film, her steps toward me were stilted as her form shifted from her own to my grandmother's to my mother's and everyone she'd apparently ever seen me interact with.

The sound of footsteps on soft dirt turned my body to stone. Niamh dropped her glamour and for a fraction of a second I thought I saw a flicker of alarm pass over her face. She watched whoever was approaching make their way over to us.

Chapter Five

"Allison?" It was Ethan's voice, full of confusion and possibly fear.

My breath stopped. What had he seen?

Don't worry Allison. I'll take care of this.

I spun around. Ethan stood with his booted feet planted firmly in the dirt. He wore his hunter green work shirt and faded blue jeans. He was staring over my shoulder at Niamh, eyes wide, like he was looking at a circus freak. And he probably thought he was.

"It's nice to finally meet you, Ethan. I'm Allison's friend Niamh. I've heard so much about you."

It was my turn to stare at Niamh wide-eyed.

I can easily convince him he never saw us.

I started to nod, hating that Ethan's mind had to be tampered with again but not knowing what else could be done.

"I don't mean to be rude, but what are you two doing back here?" Concern clouded his tone.

Niamh smiled sweetly, an odd look for her, and moved closer to him. She stared directly into his eyes and they instantly began to glaze over.

Niamh turned to me after a couple of minutes, her eyebrows scrunched together.

Something isn't right. His mind is a tangled mess.

My heart sank as I answered her with my thoughts. *What do you mean?*

My father has really outdone himself this time. I can see where he wiped out the memories of Ethan's time in Tír na n'Óg easily enough, but he's also altered Ethan's perception of you.

I looked at Ethan and swallowed thickly. His lips were slightly parted and his eyes were even more glazed-over.

Ethan's love for you is very strong, but he's been compelled to treat you as though he despises you. The two emotions are at complete odds. This isn't good.

"What are you saying? I thought you compelled people all the time. What's the big deal?"

Niamh hesitated, pursing her lips as she thought about how to answer me.

My father placed a compulsion working against Ethan's love for you. Love and loathing are battling for dominance. But no matter how much Ethan cares for you, the compulsion to be cruel to you always overrides his true feelings. If this isn't fixed, his mind could be permanently damaged.

I realized with horror what she was saying. Deaghlan had done this. He'd messed with Ethan's head on purpose. Anger seeped into my chest as I pictured the smug smile on Deaghlan's face whenever Ethan's name came up.

"You have to fix this. Fix *him.*" Fear shot through me and I couldn't keep the panic out of my voice.

I'm going to take him inside. Nobody else is here now.

I nodded, fighting back the familiar guilt. People I cared about went mad, and whether I meant for it to happen or not, it was directly related to me.

We walked into Liam's house. He'd added several pieces of furniture. An overstuffed couch, some chairs and two end tables were arranged in his living room. Niamh got Ethan to lie down on the couch without speaking a word out loud. I didn't ask how she did it.

She knelt by his head and closed her eyes as she placed her hands on his temples. Seconds ticked past as I waited for her to tell me whether she could help him or not. I started getting anxious that something was wrong when she fell back, eyes bright and chest heaving.

"Oh my god, Niamh. Are you all right?"

She blinked and turned to meet my eyes. Her placid mask slipped back into place, but not before I saw her troubled expression.

"I'm fine, it's just a more intense compulsion than I'm used to dealing with. My coercive talents aren't the strongest." She almost sounded sheepish.

She picked herself back up and put her hands back in place. The front door opened and Liam and Aodhan walked into the kitchen. I stood to meet them just as my father caught my eye.

He waited for me to come into the kitchen before he spoke. "What's up?" Hearing the expression in Liam's Irish lilt sounded so odd and I was close to losing it.

"Deaghlan messed around with Ethan's mind. Not just his memories of Tír na n'Óg, but by compelling him to be mean to me. Niamh's trying to undo the compulsion, but I think she's having some trouble."

Aodhan had his back to us, but I saw him stiffen at my words. He turned around slowly and looked from me to the living room, but didn't say anything.

Liam looked thoughtful. "Niamh doesn't have a high level of compulsion. Nothing compared to Deaghlan."

I followed Liam into the living room and stood next to the couch. Aodhan leaned against the doorway, eyebrows drawn together.

Neither Ethan nor Niamh moved when we came in. Niamh's eyes were closed tightly in concentration. The only sign that she was doing something difficult was the rapid rise and fall of her chest.

"How long has she been at it?" Liam asked.

"Too long," I said. "There was a point when she — "

Before I finished speaking, Niamh crumpled to the floor. I only saw a blur, but in an instant Aodhan was there.

I lurched forward to help, but froze when Aodhan rose fluidly with Niamh cradled in his arms.

"She just needs to rest. I'll take her to your guest room, Liam." He left the room without taking his eyes off Niamh's face.

Liam cleared his throat and raised his eyebrows at me. "Right, then. Ethan seems to be doing well, for his part."

I knelt down where Niamh had been only seconds before and softly brushed my fingers against Ethan's cheek, up to his forehead. His skin was soft and warm. I slid my hand down to check the pulse at the base of his neck — strong and healthy.

Dropping my hands to my knees, I looked up at Liam. "Physically, he seems fine. Is there any way of knowing if his mind is okay?"

"I think only time will tell," Liam said quietly.

"I tried so hard to keep him out of all this," I whispered. "I don't know how to keep everyone around me from getting hurt."

Liam sat down on the coffee table behind me. From the corner of my eye I saw him lift his hand like he would pat me on the back. His hand stopped mid-air and he put it down again.

"I know I'm not one to talk — the guilt of what I've done to your mother eats at me every day. From what I've seen, Ethan wants to be with you and I really doubt anything you would stop him. What Deaghlan did to him doesn't surprise me."

I remembered all the times Liam and Aodhan warned me that the Danaans don't feel emotions like humans. "I know. It just makes me so angry. I feel helpless and I hate it."

"Please don't berate yourself for things you can't control," he said with a tight smile. "I've spent enough time doing that for both of us."

I heard footsteps and looked up, expecting an update

from Aodhan. But it was Deaghlan who walked in. His black button down and dark jeans gave me the impression he'd been out on the town last night and was just coming in.

Liam put his hand on my shoulder and I turned. He gave me a pointed look that practically begged me to let him handle Deaghlan.

"Well isn't this a fun surprise," Deaghlan said with saccharine sweetness as he walked over to Liam's refrigerator. He pulled out a container of orange juice and sniffed it.

Liam cleared his throat, a nervous gesture. Deaghlan was intimidating, even the air around him radiated with an inhuman power.

"Deaghlan, we're having a little trouble with Allison's friend Ethan here. Seems his memories have been tampered with." I could tell he was being careful not to come right out and accuse Deaghlan of anything. No wonder he wanted to deal with him. I would have launched right into a tirade. Liam was a diplomat. I would have to remember that.

Deaghlan spun around, one eyebrow quirked up with interest. "Oh?"

I kept silent as Liam told him everything I'd said about Niamh's assessment of Ethan's mind. Not once did Deaghlan appear remorseful or bothered by anything he heard.

A slow smile played on his lips. "Well, I do hope you'll forgive me Allison. I thought you wanted to keep Ethan at a distance. Was I was mistaken?"

I looked away, my jaw clenching. "Not like this," I whispered, barely able to control the emotions flaring inside me. It grated me to cower in front of him, but I wouldn't meet his eyes. I wasn't strong enough to fight his mind tricks.

"Niamh tried to undo some of the compulsion Ethan's under, but she lost consciousness."

At Liam's words Deaghlan's eyes flashed and he cocked his head to the side, listening. "Why does she insist on being a martyr?" he mumbled before he disappeared out of the room in a blur.

"I'll never get used to that freakish speed," I said, turning back to Ethan. He hadn't moved at all. His breathing was slow and steady, barely noticeable.

Liam smiled a little, rubbing the back of his neck. "No, I suppose you won't. I'll go see how Niamh is doing, perhaps make sure Aodhan doesn't murder the king."

Looking down at Ethan, I thought about all the feelings I'd tried to deny for so long. The thrill that coursed through me whenever someone so much as mentioned his name. The way his chocolate brown eyes caused my thoughts to scatter every time he looked at me with that lopsided grin.

I traced a little pattern on his hand. His skin was smooth and warm, just like I remembered it from when he'd held my hand at his parents' Fourth of July party. That seemed so long ago, so much had happened since then. Part of me wanted him to wake up so I could be sure he was okay. But the other part was terrified that he was going to suffer for wanting to be close to me.

I felt a twitch in his finger and my eyes darted up to his face. His eyelashes fluttered open and he stared up at the ceiling for a second before he grimaced.

He moaned low in his throat and I clasped his hand so that he'd look at me. His expression was all confusion.

"It's okay, Ethan." I could feel the muscles in his abdomen tense. "Don't try to sit up, just stay quiet for a few minutes."

He faded in and out for several seconds. Whenever his eyes would open, he'd stare at me with something like fear.

People fear what they don't understand, Liam had told me more than once. Did Ethan fear me?

Did he remember seeing Niamh shift forms as he walked into Liam's backyard? And, me with her...

Ethan sat up, his eyes wide with panic as he stared at me. He was too strong for me to stop him.

"What the hell is going on?" His voice was no more than a hoarse whisper as his eyes darted around the room. "My head is… I can't even explain what is going through my mind right now."

I picked up his hand again, and I thought he would pull it out of my grasp. He just looked down at our joined hands like they held the answers to life's biggest questions in them.

I told him about the day Liam showed up on my doorstep claiming to be my father, how hard it was for me to believe anything he said . I didn't know how far to go, since I wasn't even sure what he remembered. I figured talking about being introduced to Niamh might give me an idea of whether he remembered what had happened in Liam's yard this morning.

"...and they're different from us, not just because they're inhumanly beautiful and don't age. But they have these abilities. They call it magic, but it's not like *Abracadabra* or whatever I thought magic was.

"Niamh is telepathic. She hears what I'm thinking and can speak directly into my mind. It's awful and fascinating at the same time." I forced myself to stop so I could get a feel for Ethan's reaction.

He blinked and then looked at me for a minute. He opened and closed his mouth, starting to respond and then shaking his head. Did he think I'd completely lost it?

"Liam is… Liam is your *father*?" he said, his face was twisted in confusion. I wanted nothing more than to reach up and smooth the creases that marked his forehead.

"It's okay if you don't believe me. I get it. Most days I still think I'm going crazy. And I've had a couple months to get used to it." I shook my head and tried to meet his eyes.

"No, I mean, I believe you. I saw what she did. Niamh." He said her name stiffly, like it was hard to say it out loud.

"You remember seeing her change what she looked like?"

Ethan's eyes scrunched up again and he breathed out in

a chuckle. "It was unbelievable, like I was watching some sci-fi flick where an alien morphs into a human."

I laughed, some of the tension leaving my body. "Yeah, morphing is a good word for it. They call it glamour. They can make you see or think whatever they want you to."

He thought about that for a minute without saying anything. "So Liam, your father I mean, is one of them? Does that mean you are, too?"

"No. Well, not really. He started out human. He spent a long time in their world and I guess it changed him, made him have some of their abilities. I don't think his are as strong as theirs, though. He's fast and he doesn't age, obviously. He can use glamour. But he told me glamour is a form of compulsion. And he said he can't do it as well as a true Danaan."

"I remember more than just seeing her change how she looked," Ethan said, his eyes fixed on the ceiling.

"As you've been talking I keep getting little flashes of other really weird things. I feel like I've been drunk and blacked out."

That was the part I was dreading. I couldn't imagine how many bits and pieces of his memories were floating around his mind.

"So many things have happened," I whispered, still unsure of whether he remembered Tír na n'Óg. "At one point Deaghlan wiped out a big chunk of your memories. It was supposed to be for your own good. And to keep their existence a secret, of course."

"Deaghlan?"

"He's the king of the Danaan. He's been hanging around a lot lately, mostly to cause trouble, I think."

"Is he the big, scary dude or the GQ model?"

I burst out laughing. Aodhan could definitely be described as a big, scary dude. He'd become such a good friend to me I sometimes forgot just how intimidating he was. But Ethan calling Deaghlan a GQ model was priceless.

"Deaghlan would be the GQ model," I said, snickering despite the situation. "Aodhan's a friend. He is big and scary, but he's been a great friend to me."

I told him about what had really happened when my mother had gone missing, and the more I told him, the more he remembered. He didn't remember much from Tír na n'Óg, which I was glad for because even thinking about those Danaan women touching him made me flush with something a little like anger and a lot like jealousy. Still, it felt good to have someone to say this all out loud to. Someone human. But at the same time, I was afraid of what would happen to Ethan for knowing so much.

"Do you feel well enough to stand?" I asked, wondering how much longer we had before the king himself came back down.

Ethan turned and put his feet on the floor. "I don't feel bad at all, really. Just like I could sleep for a week. What time is it anyway?"

Before I could tell him it was just a few minutes before ten, we were interrupted.

"Well, look who's awake," Deaghlan said imperiously as he entered the room.

I gritted my teeth and said nothing. Deaghlan strode over and leaned against the end of the couch Ethan was sitting on.

"If you'll excuse me, Allison. This will only take a minute or two."

"No," I said.

Deaghlan tilted his head and furrowed his brow, his eyes glinting as he looked at me.

"No?" he repeated, astonished. I doubted he heard the word very often.

"I know you think you have to wipe Ethan's memories. But I don't want you to. He won't expose you."

"Ah, Allison. I'm afraid there is no other way. Now be a good girl and give me a moment with your friend."

Ethan opened his mouth to say something, but Aodhan's voice boomed out behind us. "She said no."

Deaghlan's eyes widened and he laughed as he shook his head. "This just keeps getting better."

"Allison's right. I won't say anything," Ethan said quietly, looking between Aodhan and Deaghlan.

Deaghlan sighed. He stood up and smoothed his hands down the front of his shirt. "I regret having to go against your wishes, but as the king I often have to make difficult decisions."

With his hands held loosely behind his back, he began to pace. One look told me he lived for moments where he could display his power, like a peacock fanning his extravagant feathers.

Aodhan marched over to where I was seated on the coffee table. "Deaghlan, Allison has given you no reason to doubt her. If she says Ethan will remain silent, he will."

The look Deaghlan gave Aodhan could only be described as indulgent. I wanted to beat my fists against Deaghlan's chest and scream at him for what he'd done to Ethan. But Aodhan had warned me that despite Deaghlan's flippant appearance, he was quick to turn the switch.

"Oh, Aodhan. You have such faith in your human brethren. You weren't around when the humans rebelled against us last time. They called us monsters and came after us with their iron weapons while we slept. No, I will not trust this human, Aodhan. And you'd be wise to do the same."

Aodhan's calm facade cracked. LIghtning quick, he held Deaghlan by the throat just inches from his face.

"Don't play the fool, Deaghlan," Aodhan said, rage boiling from his gaze. "If you cared so much about your precious people, you'd be stopping Aoife from the havoc she's been wreaking. Draining humans and siphoning off their blood. Don't you know she's bringing the blood to Tír na n'Óg? Human blood with iron in it? Have you been to her place lately? Have you seen the grass won't grow, and the trees are all dying? The only things that survive in her land are black creeping vines covered in thorns."

Deaghlan's eyes narrowed and the lines of his jaw hardened as he tried to speak, but a soft voice beat him to it.

"Father," Niamh said from the entryway where she stood with Liam holding her arm. "Let go of your pride. Aodhan is trying to help.""

Aodhan sighed, releasing Deaghlan and backing away. But his eyes remained focused on the king.

"What are a dozen humans in the grand scheme of things?" Deaghlan asked with a sneer. "I just don't see what the big issue is, Aodhan."

Aodhan was quiet for a moment, seeming to weigh his answer carefully. "When your people attract media attention, doesn't that bother you? You're worried about Allison's friend knowing too much, but what if they start digging deeper in Thunder Bay?"

Deaghlan scoffed and turned his attention to me. "Nobody *there* would object to the guards wiping anyone's memories. If Aoife's guards cause trouble, Niamh has her people do damage control."

Heat rushed up my spine. Point taken, but that didn't mean I was going to sit back while he turned Ethan's mind into oatmeal. It was one thing to erase his memories, but Deaghlan had gone way beyond that.

"Now what's this about Aoife's land? I haven't heard anything about this."

Aodhan looked at Niamh, jaw clenching. I could see some silent communication going on there, which I would think more about later.

"Niamh?" Deaghlan said, giving her a look of impatience.

Niamh took a deep breath. "Breanh was teaching Aoife how to use Old Magic, as you know. Aoife hasn't been careful about keeping her guards from coming and going as they please and the effects of the iron are spreading. Plant life and animal life are dying. It's like Aodhan said, only brambles are thriving."

"What I'd like to know is why Saoirse never mentioned this to me," Deaghlan said and I wanted to punch him. It wasn't a secret that despite his feelings of grandeur when it came to humans, he enjoyed plenty of human pastimes. When he wasn't in Tír na n'Óg, he was enjoying the pleasures of this world, especially the women.

Niamh's expression shifted from plaintive to almost indignant. "Father, *everyone* has tried to tell you about this. You just don't want to hear it."

Deaghlan cast his eyes to the floor, looking thoughtful. When he looked up his expression returned to his usual blithe indifference.

"Very well, I'll play the bad guy," he said, winking at me. "It suits me."

He was playing it off, but I knew I'd seen the effect this conversation was having on him. He might act like everything was a big joke, but underneath, I was willing to bet he would finally do something about the trouble Aoife had started.

Ethan touched my arm. "If everything's cool here," he said in a hushed voice. "I really need to get back to work."

Ethan's job was waiting for him, my school work needed to get done. The real world kept spinning no matter what supernatural crises popped up, didn't it?

"Um," I said, looking around the room. "Is Ethan good to go?"

Niamh nodded, but her eyes were locked on Aodhan. Deaghlan made a gesture toward the side door, his eyes meeting mine. "By all means, but if the boy causes any problems, he'll be dealt with. No second chances."

"I'll walk you out," I said.

Ethan's truck was parked on the road at the end of Liam's driveway. We walked down without saying a word.

When the silence became too much, I glanced up at him.

He was already looking at me but I couldn't get a good grip on his expression. He squared his shoulders and if anything, I'd say he looked determined.

"I'm sorry," I said, voice wavering. "I tried to keep you out of this, I really did."

Ethan shrugged. "Nothing to be sorry about. I just need some time to process it all. But, Al?"

"Yeah?"

He opened the driver door of his pickup truck. "Whatever you're planning to do to help your parents, I want to be there."

I gaped at him. "That's not a —" He cut me off by climbing in and shutting the door.

"Good idea or not, I need you to trust me. I want to be there," he said through the open window.

Before I could respond, he started the truck and gave me a salute before driving off.

Chapter Six

I heard the screen door open and slam shut downstairs the next morning. Sticking my head out of my bedroom door, I listened for who it was.

I didn't go back to Liam's house after the showdown figuring I'd hear more from them soon enough. Instead I opted for a shower and some overdue laundry. I was actually surprised I hadn't been summoned back yet.

I heard Nicole's laughter coming from downstairs. I grabbed my cell off my bureau before I headed down.

"Hey Nic," I said when I walked into the kitchen. Nicole sat at the kitchen table with my grandmother pointing out wedding cakes in a bridal magazine. I looked across to where my mother sat in the living room watching a cooking show.

"Hey, whatcha doing?" Nicole asked without tearing her attention from the magazine.

"Not much, just finished a week's worth of laundry," I said as I sat beside her.

She turned and wrinkled her nose at me. "You're off today, right?"

"Yup, two days of good old R and R."

"Hmm, well. Want to grab a late lunch? I found some of the cutest ideas I want to show you."

I willed my face blank. I had no reason not to. I had no plans other than saving the world from blood-draining fairies. But even that seemed on hold for now.

"Yeah, lunch sounds good."

Nicole's face lit up. "Great. Let's go to The Bean Counter. I'm dying for a mocha."

We took my SUV and parked it on the street in front of Stoneville's coffee house. The place was pretty crowded, but the food was always awesome and it smelled like coffee heaven. As we entered, I gave the place a quick scan from the corner of my eye. As far as I could tell everything seemed pretty normal, no signs of glamour.

We seated ourselves and opened our menus. The sound of a couple arguing a few tables over caught my attention. A girl with spiky black hair sat with her back to us. Across from her, a tall guy with caramel-colored hair around our age sat fiddling with a straw wrapper, but his demeanor was agitated.

I went back to my menu and decided to order a turkey club and a mocha Frappuccino. Once the waitress took our orders, Nicole pulled a stack of magazines out of her messenger bag.

I bit back any comments, because this was Nicole's big dream and I wasn't about to ruin it for her. She had little post-it notes marking up dozens of pages and we pored over them until our food arrived.

While we ate, I absently noted the arguing couple getting up to leave. I glanced over and when I got a look at the girl's face, I gasped.

She looked just like Aoife.

But it wasn't her. Her chin length black hair framed her face in perfectly arranged spikes. Aoife's hair was long waves down her back. This girl had piercings covering both ears and in her eyebrow and lip. I would have remembered if Aoife had multiple piercings.

When the guy she was with caught her looking at me, he grabbed her elbow and pushed her toward the door. She went without arguing, but not before taking one more curious glance at me. I watched them out of the corner of my eye as they made their way out the front door.

I tried to focus on what Nicole was saying about linen chair covers, but I couldn't get the girl's face out of my mind. It had been almost an exact match. Maybe her cheeks were a little fuller, but still, so close.

My mind was going over the idea that maybe it was Aoife and she was glamoured to look human. But that didn't make sense. I'd looked for glamour and there was none.

I made a few affirmative noises to Nicole, not really surprised she didn't notice my distraction. She was in her element with all the planning involved in a wedding.

When our food arrived, the couple was still standing outside the plate glass window at the front The Bean Counter. The girl gestured widely with her hands while the guy stood with his arms crossed. He glanced over and saw me watching. I averted my eyes for a second, but when I looked back, they were gone. They disappeared into thin air.

I unwrapped my straw and plunged it into my Frappuccino. My mind was reeling with the possibilities. I couldn't wait to get out of there, but I wasn't sure who I should talk to. Liam? If my suspicions were true and this girl was Samantha, he might not be the best one. I still hadn't told him he might have another daughter, one whose mother happened to be Aoife. Niamh seemed a better bet. Although I didn't know if she'd brush this aside because of everything else going on.

"Allison."

I started at the sound of my name. "Hmm?" I said between sips.

"I said I need to get a dress for the engagement party next weekend. Will you come?"

"Yeah, I will. But can we do it tomorrow? I have a ton of homework this weekend."

Nicole sighed, but nodded. "How is school? You don't say much about it."

"It's good, but there's a lot of work." I took a bite of my

sandwich so I didn't have to elaborate. The topic of homework made Nicole's eyes glaze over. She'd gone to beauty school right after high school and had been working full-time for years.

"Okay, so I'm glad you like the invitations. Mom wasn't sure if they were elegant enough, but I want everything to be stylish and fun, not some stuffy, traditional wedding."

"No, they were great," I said, plastering on my brightest smile.

The waitress came with the bill and Nicole snatched it up from me. "You've endured all this wedding talk, let it be my treat."

Guilt ate at me. I'd only heard a quarter of what she said, but I couldn't stand to take away her happiness. I nodded and, once again, pulled out my cousin-of-the-year smile.

I tried paying attention while Nicole was trying on dress after dress at the mall the next day, but my mind was on the black-haired girl at The Bean Counter. Thankfully Nic talked herself out of each one with only a few nods needed from me.

She inspected herself in the mirror, spinning for full effect. While she looked at her back, frown lines popped up between her eyebrows. "You know, I think you should try this on. It's too long for me, but I bet the color would really bring out your eyes."

"Me?" I said, startled. "All right, I'll try it." I had to get something for the engagement party anyway, I might as well go with one pre-approved by the bride-to-be.

I went into the dressing room next to hers, the ice blue dress in hand. The neckline was a little more daring than I was used to, but Nic was right, the color did bring out my eyes.

I stepped out to show her and as I scanned the dressing area I caught the faintest silver shimmer in the doorway. I blinked and the shape of a girl melted into view.

My eyes snapped open, shocked to see the girl from yesterday standing less than ten feet away. My surprise must have registered on my face because when I looked at her, her eyes widened in panic and she bolted from the dressing area.

"Wait," I called out, but she was gone before I could make it to the doorway. I cursed under my breath at my bare feet and unpaid dress. I couldn't chase after her like this.

"What in the world are you doing?" Nic said from behind me. I spun around, heat creeping up my neck.

"Oh, I just thought I saw a girl from school," I said, looking down at my bare toes.

"I was right, that dress is perfect for you," she said, changing the subject.

"Thanks," I said, tilting my head at the shell pink chiffon dress she had on. "Wasn't that the first dress you tried on?"

"Yes," she said, scrunching up her face at her reflection. "And I don't know. I think I like this one best after all."

I couldn't help grinning. "It's perfect, you look amazing."

After I changed, Nicole decided to try on one more dress, just to be sure. I pulled my phone out and stared at it. Should I call Niamh and tell her about the girl?

I decided to send her a text. That would give me an idea of her reaction without having to talk in code.

I have something to tell you.

She replied before I could even put my phone back in my pocket.

Are you still at the mall?

I told her I was and to watch for me in about half an hour.

As Nicole and I paid for our dresses, I wondered if I'd made the right decision. Maybe I shouldn't tell Niamh yet. I just wasn't sure.

When we got back home Nicole grabbed her bag from my trunk and said goodbye before she darted next door. On Sunday's there was always a big dinner at the Magliaro residence. Since Nicole thought Ethan and I still weren't speaking, she didn't even beg me to come with her.

I climbed the steps onto my front porch feeling a little paranoid. What if Samantha was somewhere out there watching me right now?

The hall clock just inside the front door said it was just after two. I'd hang up my dress and go for a walk next door to talk to Niamh and still have plenty of time to finish up my homework.

"I'm home," I called down the hall, not sure who was around. I could hear the sound of studio audience laughter from the television and just made out my mother's feet tucked under her on the couch in the living room at the end of the hallway.

"Allison, we're back here. You have company," Gram said, and I heard plates being moved around and footsteps on the kitchen tiles.

I tossed my bag on the stairs and went down the hall to see who it could be. When I got to the kitchen, surprise flitted through me. Niamh sat at the kitchen table drinking tea with Gram. I glanced over at my mother who just stared at the television, like she was completely oblivious to the Danaan in our house. I knew she wasn't, she'd told me once in Tír na n'Óg that she was still aware of everything around her, she just couldn't show it.

"Hey," I said, raising an eyebrow at Niamh.

I introduced myself as Liam's sister. Go along with it.

"Did you find something pretty at the mall, sweetheart?" Gram asked before raising her tea cup to her lips.

"I did. Well, Nicole picked it out, actually."

Gram laughed. "So, Niamh tells me you two have a couple of classes together?"

Say yes.

"Yes, we do." I cleared my throat and looked at Niamh. "Isn't that such a coincidence?"

"It really is," Gram said. "Such a small world."

"Absolutely." Niamh turned to me. "I was hoping you had those notes from Friday for me to look at."

"Oh, yeah sure. They're just upstairs, come on."

I hurried up the stairs, Niamh trailing behind me. Once the door was closed I sat on my bed Niamh looked at me expectantly and I bit my lip.

I thought about the girl I'd seen, imagined her face and dark hair in my mind for Niamh to see.

You've seen Samantha too, I take it?

Surprised she put it together so quick, I just blinked at her.

Yes, I knew about Samantha.

I shook my head. *But Aoife acted like it was a big secret.*

She doesn't realize I know about her child. There are many things Aoife doesn't know.

Does Liam know?

Niamh walked over and sat in my desk chair. *No.*

Why haven't you told him?

Remember, there's a significant time difference between my world and yours, Allison.

To me, it's only been just over a year since Aoife gave birth to Samantha. And in between that time, many things happened that kept me from telling Liam. By then, he had discovered he had you. It just hasn't been the right time.

I shot her a sidelong look as something else occurred to me. *You said 'I saw Samantha too.' Does that mean you've seen her?*

I sensed them before I saw them. I can tell when my people are nearby, and Ciarán, the Danaan she's with, knows this. I think he's humoring Samantha by letting her think she's sneaking around on us. She's not sure how to approach you or Liam yet. But I do know from her thoughts that she doesn't mean you any harm.

Good. I breathed a sigh of relief. Images of Samantha killing me in my sleep had been dancing in my head since lunch yesterday.

Samantha has a significant amount of Danaan blood. She's a telepath like me. As you might guess, it's given her a great deal of trouble in this world

I imagined what it must be like to hear people's thoughts. Even the dreams I had made me think I was crazy. She must have had it much worse.

So she's my half-sister?

Niamh smiled, wrapping a strand of hair around her finger. *Yes, that's right.*

I wasn't sure how to feel about that. I had a sister. She looked right around my age, too. But something felt off. Like Niamh was holding back. I wished I hadn't thought that when her eyes lifted to mine.

I've scanned her thoughts, which is more difficult than just hearing thoughts. I know Aoife has been to see her, but I haven't been able to figure out what Aoife is up to. Which is why I've kept quiet about it. Diarmuid, my adviser, thought it best to wait until we had a better understanding of the situation before telling Liam.

Okay, so Samantha met Aoife and she told her about all of us. I guess I could understand she was curious about meeting her father. Not only that, but Niamh was her aunt and I was her sister. What I couldn't put my finger on was why Aoife had gone to meet her after keeping her a secret for twenty-odd years, or just over a year in her own world. Why now?

Those are the same things I'd like to know.

How do we get her to talk to us?

My father has the ability to call Ciarán out. Nobody, Danaan or human, can resist his compulsion.

A shudder rolled through my body. How ironic that the thing that made Deaghlan so repulsive was exactly what we needed.

He plans to go back to Tír na n'Óg today to take stock of the damage done from the iron, but we may be able to have him help us before he leaves.

Are you going back too?

I haven't decided. I should go. I need to talk to my mother about so many things. And I'm weak from reversing my father's work on Ethan's mind. But I'm not sure if it's a good idea to leave now.

Before I could stop myself I wondered if that was because of Samantha or because Aodhan was here and she didn't want risk losing track of him.

Niamh looked sort of amused. *Both.*

How do you think Liam is going to take the news?

Good question. Shall we go find out?

Chapter Seven

I felt terrible adding another lie to the dozens I'd told my grandparents lately. But letting them think Niamh was Liam's sister seemed a much better choice than the truth. Would I ever be able to have that conversation with them?

Gram and Pop, Liam is actually my dad. You know, the one who knocked Mom up back in Ireland? I know he looks my age, that's just because he's spent so long in a magical fairy world, cursed so he couldn't come be with Mom. Oh, and Niamh isn't his sister, she's really a fairy princess from the other world. Her crazy sister Aoife is an evil fairy who steals human blood to make her more powerful. It's her fault Mom lost her mind, so don't blame Liam, okay?

No, lying was the way to go.

With a sigh I told Gram I'd see her in a couple hours and that Niamh and I were going to watch a movie next door.

We found Liam stretched out on a lawn chair in his backyard with his eyes closed. I hesitated when I imagined how our news would turn his life upside down. Again.

Niamh turned to look at me and squeezed my shoulder. It was such a human gesture, I almost laughed. Maybe there was hope for their race after all.

"Hey old man," I said, nudging his chair with my foot.

Liam opened one eye and looked over at me. "How right you are," he said. He sat up and rubbed a hand over his face.

"Liam, we have some news," Niamh said as she pulled

two more lawn chairs over.

I sat on the chair she offered me. Liam looked between us as I pulled my legs up and wrapped my arms around them.

"Before we captured Aoife in Tír na n'Óg, do you remember a time when she was gone for longer than usual?"

He raised an eyebrow. "Gone? Well, a few times that she left for what seemed longer than others. Why do you ask?"

"From what I can gather, it was right around the time you met Elizabeth. She came to this realm, alone. She stayed here for nearly a year without returning home to you. Of course it would have felt like little more than a week to you."

"Yes, I suppose I remember. At that point I was able to see Elizabeth every few days. Why?"

"Well, during that time, Aoife had a secret she was keeping from all of us."

"Just one?" Liam asked dryly.

"One in particular," Niamh said. She drew in her lips and looked at her lap for a moment. "Liam, Aoife became pregnant with your child. She didn't want the baby, afraid you would love it more than you loved her. So she made Eithne hide her in this world."

Liam stood. "My child?" His hands flew to his hair so fast they blurred. "That's not possible, I would have known…"

"There's a lot of that going on lately, huh?" I said and wished I could stick my foot in my mouth.

Niamh chuckled softly. "There's more. Your other child, your daughter, has come looking for you. From what I've read of the girl's thoughts, Aoife found her living in Thunder Bay. She knows about you and about Allison."

He laughed, a small desperate sound. His hair stood up at odd angles from the abuse he was inflicting on it as he paced back and forth.

"I don't know what to say.. What am I supposed to do?" His words all melted into one another.

"Liam, it's okay. We're going to talk to her. Figure out what she's doing here," I said as I reached for his wrists, trying to get him to stop before he pulled all his hair out.

"How long have you known about this?" he asked Niamh.

"Does that matter right now?" Niamh asked, neatly deflecting him. "What's more important is finding out any information she has about Aoife, wouldn't you agree?"

"Yes, yes. I suppose you're right." He ran a hand down his face.

"Okay. She has one of Aoife's guards with her. You remember Ciarán?"

Liam nodded, but kept his hand over his eyes. "Is he another murderous fiend now, draining humans?"

"I don't know. I can't get past his mind shields. But he doesn't look haggard like Aengus does in your memories."

The image of the guard who attacked Liam and me in Thunder Bay, like a walking cadaver, popped into my head. When Liam and Niamh imprisoned Aoife, her guards had become addicted to the small bits of magic in human blood.

"Good to know the girl isn't traveling with the likes of him," Liam said.

Niamh shifted in her seat next to me. "We're going to try to get my father draw Ciarán out. After that, I'll be going home to speak with my mother."

"Good, good." Liam said. He started walking toward his back door. "I'm just going to get a drink of water." His hair stuck out like a porcupine and his skin was a ghastly white. He was spooked, discovering he had two daughters in two months.

I slapped my hands down on my thighs. "That went well."

Niamh glanced from me to the back door. "About as well as expected."

My phone buzzed in my pocket. It was a text from Ethan. My insides tightened.

Just finished dinner, wish you came. You busy?

I laughed to myself. Was I busy? I was sitting in my father's backyard waiting for him to lose it after learning he had not just one, but two grown daughters.

Despite that, I felt a little warm and fuzzy inside. He wished I came to dinner?

I replied, *Just talking to Liam and Niamh. What's up?*

Nothing much. Just checking in. Text me when you're free.

You got it.

Ethan wanted me to text him. No matter what happened, he never gave up on me.

I felt a strange feeling of inevitability, like maybe I'd always known one day we'd end up together and I'd just been a fool. I looked at Liam's back door, thinking maybe that's what love was. Liam hadn't given up on my mother even after everything Aoife put him through. Maybe love meant believing in someone so much, no obstacle in this world or the next could change your mind.

"I hope you're right," Niamh said. She stood up and motioned for me to do the same. "Let's give Liam a moment. We can check on him later."

"Okay," I said, following her out of the yard toward the front of the house. "I have tons of homework I need to finish for school tomorrow anyway.

She nodded. "I'm going up to Wheelwright to see if I can catch my father. If you need me, just call me and I can be back here immediately."

Just as it started getting dark out, I finished my homework and laid my head down on my desk, rolling my neck to stretch the muscles. My cell phone next to my desk lamp caught my eye, so I picked it up and reread the text from

Ethan.

I tried to think of something witty to say, but nothing came to me. I'd learned in psychology that people respond best to questions about themselves, so I figured that was a good place to start.

How was dinner?

Dinner was good. Would have been better if you came.

Sorry. Lots of homework.

Homework? Guess that's better than 'washing your hair'.

Haha very funny.

How are things?

Everything's good, you?

Instead of texting me back, the phone rang. When I pressed talk, Ethan didn't even give me a chance to say hello.

"I realized where I went wrong with you, you know."

"Well, hello to you too," I said.

"No, listen for a sec. When we were…" he trailed off. "Before, I tried to get your attention by doing what always worked with other girls. Flirting, teasing, that sort of thing. So now I know that's where I went wrong."

I shook my head. "Okaaaay."

"It makes sense, doesn't it? I've been thinking about it. You're not like other girls, so why would you react like them? You wouldn't."

"Ethan—"

"Come on, Al. I know I'm right. I've decided I'm going to change my approach. We'll be friends, if that's what you want. But you're going to have to trust me. Do you trust me?"

"Of course…"

"Uh uh, tell me you trust me."

"I trust you."

"Good. Now, when I ask you 'How are things?' don't give me some lame answer like "oh fine," or try to change the subject. You trust me, so tell me how things really are.

Tell me about… what you did today. Or what's new with your mom and dad. Talk to me."

I took a deep breath. "Well, my mom is okay. She's been writing music. Writing songs like she did before, you know?"

"Really? That's awesome." he said. "What about Liam?"

I sighed. "Liam is… I don't know. Liam's fine."

"You're doing it again. What happened after we left Friday?"

"Oh, man. I don't even know what happened with Deaghlan." So much had happened. Seeing the girl at The Bean Counter and the mall.

"Is that normal? I got the impression you talk to Liam a lot."

"No, you're right. I talk to him all the time. It's just…something else happened." It was so strange talking to Ethan about this. I was finding it hard to put everything into words. But at the same time it felt sort of amazing to have someone I could talk to about it.

"Are you all right?"

"I'm fine, yeah." I licked my lips, trying to think of how to say it. "When Nic and I went out for lunch yesterday, there was this girl there. She looked so much like Aoife that I thought for a second I was done for. I mean, she could have just…I don't know, killed me or compelled me or something."

"Did she do anything to you?"

"What? No. I snapped out of it and realized it wasn't Aoife. But I know she has a daughter and this was her. She was following me." I had to take a deep breath. My heart was racing just remembering.

"Aoife is the one who put the curse on your…on Liam?"

"Yeah. I guess she had a baby, Liam's baby, and never even told him. I don't really understand how it all worked out. But she's here in Stoneville for some reason. And we had to tell Liam today. I think he's still in shock. Well he was when I left his house earlier."

"Listen, is it okay if I come over?"

"Yeah. I mean, of course."

"Okay, give me ten minutes and I'll be there."

He hung up and I just stared at the phone, dumbstruck. Ethan was being my friend. He wanted me to trust him. Just last week he'd been giving me the cold shoulder and this was… My shoulders slumped. Who was I kidding? This was exactly what I needed.

I put my enormous statistics textbook and binder into my backpack. I was grateful I had this weekend off, or I'd never have been able to keep up with my homework. Maybe Gram was right, maybe I did need to consider taking some time off from work.

I went downstairs, walked into the living room and froze. Liam was sitting on the couch in between my mother and Gram.

Pop was in his recliner laughing at something Liam was telling Gram. My mother was staring at his hands as he gestured while he spoke. She looked completely at ease.

"Hey Liam," I said, glancing between him and my grandmother.

"Oh, hello Allison. I was just telling your grandmother about the squirrel at my bird feeder. The little rascal isn't leaving any seed for the birds."

My brows rose. "Really? Poor birds." I shook my head. He sure knew how to charm my grandparents. They could go on for hours about birds and what happened at the feeders.

"I'm just going for a walk, get some fresh air. I have my phone if you need me," I said, smiling.

"I'd love a walk. Mind if I join you?" Liam stood, his hand lifting to pat my mother's knee. Because of the geis Aoife placed on him, he wasn't able to touch her. It was as if his hand hit an invisible force field and he dropped it before backing away.

"Lovely to see you Mrs. O'Malley, Mr. O'Malley. Elizabeth." He nodded and spun on his heel before following me to the door.

Once the door had shut behind us, I laughed and sat down on the porch steps "They'll try to adopt you if you talk bird watching with them."

"Oh, that? Well, I'm glad they like me." Liam walked down the steps and turned back to face me. "It's…wonderful just to be near your mother."

A feeling of calm spread over me and I felt myself smiling.

"Ethan's on his way over. I haven't really talked to him since Friday."

Liam ran a hand over his hair and blew out a sigh. "Do you think he's okay with things?"

"Define 'okay.' I mean, he seems to be fine. He doesn't think I'm crazy at least."

"That's good. I'm sorry about my behavior earlier," he said, sinking down next to me. As you might imagine it came as quite a shock."

"Yeah, I'm sure it did. I just wish we knew what Samantha wants. I guess we'll find out soon enough."

"I would imagine she wants what anyone would want. To know why her father was never around." He covered his face with his hands and shook his head.

"Hey, I came around didn't I?" I said, nudging his shoulder. "We'll make sure she understands."

A small, sad smile appeared on his lips. "I'm quite glad you did. I'm just so damn angry. I want to put an end to all this madness. But it seems like there's always something more she's done. I'm caught in Aoife's spider web and I can't see how I'll ever be free."

Headlights peeked through the night and Ethan's truck pulled up in front of the house. The sound of his truck door opening and slamming shut echoed in the quiet evening. Even dressed in a plain white T-shirt and worn jeans he looked amazing. He shoved his hands in his pockets and walked over to where we sat.

I smiled as I stood up and rubbed my arms. "Hey."

Ethan gave me a little smile and I felt my heart turn over. Liam stood and they shook hands.

"What's going on?" Ethan said, looking between us.

"Not much," I said, glancing at Liam out of the corner of my eye.

"How are you handling everything?" Liam asked.

Ethan chuckled. "Well, I guess I'm still processing it. I probably wouldn't believe it if I hadn't seen it with my own eyes."

Liam jerked his chin toward his house. "Shall we go where we can talk?"

I watched Ethan follow behind Liam and I trailed a few steps behind them. Liam opened his front door, motioning for us to go in first. It was dark and quiet inside. Our steps echoed on the tiles of his foyer.

"Where's Aodhan?" I asked Liam when we were all sitting in his living room. "I haven't seen him around in a couple days."

"He went for a hike at the state park Friday. He hasn't been back since. I think he's getting restless."

"I'm not surprised," I said, trying to imagine what he could be doing for the past two days in the wilderness. It was probably relaxing to be away from all of this. He didn't have to worry about being attacked by a bear or anything. He could outrun any animal and fight off any predator.

"How does Aodhan fit into all of this, anyway?" Ethan asked, rubbing his jaw.

Liam looked thoughtful for a minute. "Aodhan and Niamh were once in love. She brought him home with her after he'd been shot by a British soldier in the early seventeenth century. He stayed in Tír na n'Óg for so long that everyone he cared about was long gone by the time he came back here."

Ethan shifted in his seat on the couch, his knee pressing into mine. All thought left me, and my mind focused on that one spot where we were connected.

"That's harsh. So they're not together anymore?" he asked, meeting my eyes.

I blinked and glanced over at Liam, thinking back to the time in Thunder Bay when I'd asked him the same question. I hadn't understood the dynamic between Niamh and Aodhan back then, not that I fully grasped it now.

Liam took a deep breath and let it out slowly. "They're not. Things between them are complicated. I'm sure you'll figure that out pretty quickly if you plan on sticking around."

A hot flush crept over my cheeks, spreading down my neck. I looked down at my hands clasped in my lap, peeking up through my lashes to make out Ethan's reaction. He bumped my knee with his, amusement flickering in his deep brown eyes.

"Have you heard anything from Niamh?" I asked, trying to focus on the bigger issue at hand.

My sister. Not Ethan's dimples.

Liam frowned. "Not yet, she sent a message that she was in Wheelwright.."

"What's she doing up there?" Ethan asked.

"She has a house. It's where one of the portals to Tír na n'Óg is." I studied Ethan's reaction. He just nodded, taking it in stride.

The front door slammed shut and, as if we had summoned her, Niamh walked into the living room. Her face was expressionless, but her posture was rigid.

"My father's gone. He went to Tír na n'Óg without me," she said, crossing her arms.

"What happened?" Liam asked, standing.

"Diarmuid said he came up there on Friday ranting about us allowing Ethan to keep his memories and Aoife destroying Tír na n'Óg."

"It's about time he starts taking what she's done

seriously," Liam said.

"Yes. I just wish I could've caught him before he left. It would have made it easier to deal with Ciarán and Samantha." Niamh tapped her finger on her lips and looked at me. "Have you seen them again?"

I shook my head. "Not since I was at the mall."

Ethan squeezed my knee and when I looked at him, he gave me a reassuring smile.

"I'd like to find them tonight," Niamh said, her eyes on Liam.

Liam nodded. "If that's what you think is best," he said, but he grew pale and his jaw tightened.

I swallowed, unnerved by his reaction. This was happening fast, it was possible we could have answers to Aoife's whereabouts tonight. *Or someone could get hurt*, a tiny voice whispered in my head.

"I do." Niamh's gaze focused on me. "And Allison, Samantha doesn't mean you any harm. I know that much."

I wanted to be brave. It wasn't so much that I was scared of Samantha, more I was afraid of what we'd find out. What if the hope we had of setting my mother free from her mental prison was taken away?

"Okay," I said, willing my fear away. "What do we have to do?"

"I'm going to call to Samantha, speak into her mind. Then we'll wait and see if she responds."

Niamh gestured to the backdoor. "It'll be easier outside."

I got up to follow her out when Ethan placed his hand on my shoulder. I turned and his eyes searched mine. "You okay?" he asked.

"Yeah, I'm fine. Just nervous," I said with a weak smile.

"Come on, I want to see what Niamh can do," he said, wrapping his arm around my waist and pulling me toward the door.

Outside, Liam sat beside Niamh in the chairs we'd been

in earlier. He watched as she rubbed her temples, her eyes closed in concentration.

The minutes ticked by before Niamh sat up and ran a hand over her eyes. We all watched her, waiting to hear what happened.

"She and Ciarán are coming here now."

Liam blinked at Niamh, and then his gaze flicked up to mine.

"That's it? She didn't resist you at all?" I asked.

Niamh stood and smoothed the front of her slim black pants. "She was very eager, as a matter of fact."

Liam ran his hands through his hair and stood up. "This is good, isn't it? She wants to meet me." A nervous smile was on his face as he looked around.

"Try to be cool, Liam." I said, hoping to ease his tension.

He laughed, rubbing his hands over his face. "Be cool. Right, I can do that." The words seemed funny coming from Liam, with his old-fashioned manners.

"Remember Allison," Niamh said. "Samantha doesn't know our side of things yet. Let's hear what she has to say before we tell them anything."

I nodded. "Of course."

"Just follow my lead and everything will be fine," she said, looking between the three of us.

Chapter Eight

The sound of footsteps in the gravel driveway took me by surprise. The Danaan moved so fast and soundlessly, I'd expected Samantha and Ciarán to appear out of thin air.

Ciarán came into view first. He held his hands out in front of him. "I'm unarmed," he said in a level voice.

Niamh nodded, waiting for him to approach. He glanced over his shoulder and nodded.

Samantha stepped into the moonlight, her arms wrapped around herself, her hair so black it almost shone blue. Her steps were tremulous, I could almost feel the range of emotions coming from her. Excitement, nervousness and anxiety swirled around her. Ciarán eyed each of us through the thick fringe of his shaggy hair.

"Welcome, Samantha, Ciarán," Niamh said, her voice lacking any real emotion.

"Hey," Samantha said in a husky voice, one hand shooting up in a jerky wave before she wrapped it back around her middle. Ciarán didn't speak, just nodded

"Samantha," Liam said, the name sounding stiff and unnatural.

Samantha drew in her lips, toying with the little ball of her labret piercing.

I stepped forward, offering my hand. "I'm Allison, and this is my friend Ethan. It's really great to meet you."

Ethan shook her hand and offered to shake Ciarán's

hand, but he just looked at Ethan's outstretched palm.

Samantha nudged Ciarán. "You're supposed to take his hand and shake it," she whispered, rolling her eyes.

"No big deal," Ethan said, pulling back his hand and smiling.

"W-would you like to come inside?" Liam asked, rubbing his hand over the back of his neck.

Samantha exchanged a look with Ciarán and he nodded. "Okay," she said, bouncing on the balls of her feet.

Liam held the door as everyone walked into his living room.

Samantha sat in one of the armchairs, her black suede boots tapping a machine-gun staccato on the wooden floor. Ciarán leaned on the armrest gazing off into the distance, arms crossed.

Ethan and I sat across from them on the couch. Liam stood behind me, his hands braced on the back of the couch. I bit my lip as the room reached an extreme level of awkwardness. Nothing could have prepared me for this moment and now that it was here, I couldn't think of how to say the things I wanted.

As I thought that, Samantha's eyes darted to mine.

Can you hear me? I thought.

Her blue eyes narrowed and I held my breath. She seemed to weigh her answer before she nodded.

Niamh moved from behind the couch to stand where we could all see her. She held her hands behind her back, facing Samantha and Ciarán.

"We're very glad you agreed to meet with us," she said. "I'd like to get right to the point and ask what brings you here, what your intentions are?"

Samantha fidgeted in her seat and licked her lips. "Well, the whole having a father and sister thing was kind of intriguing, you know?"

Unable to help it, I laughed. "I know *exactly* what you mean."

"Right?" she said, laughing too.

"Of course," Niamh said giving me a cool, measured look. "But what I'd really like to know is whether Aoife asked you to come here."

Samantha flinched, probably because of Niamh's directness. It wasn't in her nature to be subtle.

"No," Samantha said, eyebrows drawn down low. "I don't even know what she wanted from me. It was like, maybe, I disappointed her or something. Once she met me, she couldn't get away from me fast enough."

Ciarán glanced down at her, his jaw clenching. "It wasn't like that, Sam," he said quietly, but Samantha didn't look convinced.

Liam cleared his throat behind me. "If there's one thing I know about Aoife, it's that she is an entirely selfish creature. Whatever her reason for wanting to meet you, chances are they were purely for her own benefit."

"I have my own ideas about why she would want to meet you," I said. I was met with varying expressions of interest.

"I met Aoife mostly by accident," I said, meeting Samantha's eyes. "The only reason I knew you existed was because she thought I was you. She even called me Samantha."

"This is news to me," Liam said.

"I know, but just hear me out. She was stressed because she thought Liam would find out she'd kept his child a secret. She wanted to send 'Samantha' back home before Liam discovered what she'd done. When she realized I wasn't you, and that Liam had another daughter, I think she decided you might make a useful weapon she could use to bring Liam back."

Liam scoffed. "How would that work?"

"Well, she knows your sense of responsibility. You said it yourself -- she's selfish. Is she selfish enough to use her own child as bait to lure you back to her?"

"Oh, I see. You might be right, Allison," Liam said.

Niamh didn't say anything, she just stood still. I wondered what she made of this.

Without meeting my eyes she said, "I think you're right. That sounds just like what Aoife would do."

"So, what did she say to you while you were together?" I asked Samantha.

"Well, at first she asked a lot of questions about my... abilities," Samantha said, toying with one of the rings on her finger. She looked up and met my eyes. "She wanted to know about the voices I hear."

Before she could continue, Ciarán stood up. "There's something you should know," he said in a low voice. "I don't think Aoife came looking for Sam."

Samantha looked up at Ciarán, pursing her lips.

"Why don't you think so?" I said.

"Aoife showed up at the house, troubled about something. She wouldn't tell us what happened, but she had this hunted look, like someone was after her. The next day, Sam showed up and Aoife knew instantly who she was."

"How is it possible that of all the people in the world, you end up with Aoife's daughter?" I asked Ciarán, skeptical that it was merely a coincidence.

"Nobody is more surprised by that than I am," Ciarán said.

"Ciarán and I met almost a year ago," Samantha said, cutting him off. "I used to go and watch him and the guys play. I didn't know anything about the Tuatha de Danaan or magic. I just loved their music."

"We had a band, Finn, Seamus, me and Aengus," Ciarán said. "I didn't even know she was Aoife's daughter until a few weeks ago. I knew she had Danaan blood, though. It was what drew me to her."

Samantha rolled her eyes.

"But you're Aoife's guard. Why should we trust you?"

It's the truth, Allison. Niamh told me in my thoughts. She raised her hand to Ciarán, signaling him to wait.

"Okay, so then what?" I said.

"She was making preparations for something. She refused to tell us what she was up to, though," Ciarán said, looking away.

"That's why I wanted to come here," Samantha said, a pinched look on her face. "I think she's going to do something to you, Liam."

Liam laughed grimly. "Not that I'm surprised, but what makes you say that?"

"I overheard her talking on the phone about going to Ireland and a binding. I didn't understand all she was saying, but I'm pretty sure I heard your name. "

"Binding?" I said, making a face, but nobody responded.

Niamh started to pace the length of the living room. Her eyes were unfocused and I wasn't sure if she was reading someone's thoughts or just trying to sort out everything they'd told us.

Moonlight coming in through the windows illuminated Liam's pale face. He stared at the floor, his fingers twisted into his hair.

"Are we talking about binding as in tying someone up?" I had a feeling it was much more than that, but I had to ask.

Niamh stopped pacing and gave me a bland look. "No. Binding in this case would be a form of old magic. It can be used for good, for protection and so on. But I have a feeling that's not what Aoife is up to."

"And what are the 'not so good' things it can be used for?" I asked, my voice small.

"Well," Niamh said, glancing at Liam. "It can also be used to seal someone's fate."

I swallowed, understanding setting in. "But Liam would have to be with her for that to happen, right?"

Liam and Niamh were both quiet for a second. Liam cleared his throat and met my eyes. "Not necessarily. She has my blood, that's enough to perform a binding."

I looked around the room and jumped up. "No. That can't happen. My mother needs you."

Ethan stood beside me, placing a hand on my arm. The warmth of his skin grounded me and I took a breath, trying to calm down.

Liam tilted his head to the side and blinked. "I'm not giving up, if that's what you think."

I shook my head. "I'm... sorry. I didn't mean it like that. I know you're not."

Samantha and Ciarán hadn't said anything as Niamh gave me a lesson in magical binding. I looked at Ciarán and before I could stop myself I asked, "Do *you* think that's what she's planning?"

Ciarán pressed his lips into a thin line. "Yes. She placed the geis on Liam, thinking he'd forget the human if he couldn't be with her. She now realizes it wasn't enough."

Samantha sniffed and looked at Liam and then me. "I know we don't know each other, but I'd want someone to tell me."

My hands shook a little as I sat back down. Ethan sat by my side, his thigh pressed against mine. "Could she do this binding at any time?"

Niamh shook her head. "Binding magic isn't a simple process. There are a lot of pieces to set in motion. It could take months to prepare."

Relief flooded through me. I was imagining a switch flipping and Liam turning into another version of my mother, desperately longing for Aoife.

"This is good, right? I mean, at least we have something to go on. I was going crazy waiting for her to make her next move." I looked at Liam who was staring out into the night sky, his expression shuttered.

Anger flashed in Liam's eyes when he glanced over at me, but he tamped it down quickly.

He opened his mouth to speak, but closed it again, shaking his head.

"Allison has a point," Niamh said, moving to stand by Liam's side. "We knew she wouldn't let it go."

"I want… I want to kill her for this," Liam whispered, swallowing thickly as he turned back to the window.

Part of me was shocked at this side of Liam. But I could understand how he felt. A small, dark part of me wished I'd killed her in Tír na n'Óg.

"If she were to die, what would happen with the geis?" I asked.

Niamh stared at me for several long minutes. "If she died, the geis would be wiped away."

But, Allison? She is still my sister and I'd like to solve this without ending her life.

I nodded briefly, knowing she'd feel that way. "I wish we could talk to Saoirse and find out what she knows."

"I leave tonight for Tír na n'Óg," Niamh said. "With the time difference, I can be back in as soon as a few days."

"But when we were there for what seemed like a few days, it turned out to be more than a month," I said.

"That's right, but I meant I could be back in a few of your days, which would be just a few hours there."

"And if you're gone longer?" I asked.

Niamh smiled. "That will just mean there's no rush after all."

Ethan and I walked to my house in silence. He stopped at the bottom of the porch steps. I looked down at him. "You want to come in?"

He beamed at me like I'd offered him a slice of chocolate cake. "I would, unless you need some time alone?"

I shook my head. "Actually, I *don't* want to be alone right now."

I went inside, making sure not to make too much noise

so I didn't wake anyone up. Ethan followed me down the hall to the kitchen. I grabbed two sodas from the fridge and sat at the table beside him.

"You okay?" he asked.

I shrugged and wiped at the condensation on the soda can. "Yeah, I think so."

He reached over and cupped my hand, pulling it away from the soda. "Come on, talk to me."

"I'm trying," I said and took a deep breath. "But it isn't something that comes easy for me." My voice trailed off, barely a whisper.

I watched as he lightly brushed his fingers over my hand. His gaze flicked up to mine. "I know. I'm not trying to push you."

I nodded. "Trusting is... hard for me, too. I didn't want to trust Liam or any of them. But I ended up with no choice. Now with Samantha and Ciarán, I don't know what to think."

"You mean you think they're up to something?" he asked.

I sighed. "No. I don't know, not really. But if *I* hadn't known my mother my whole life and she showed up, I know I'd want her to like me. I'd want to impress her. I wouldn't blame Samantha if she was trying to help Aoife. But it would *really* suck."

"I was thinking the same thing, but you said Niamh can read minds. Wouldn't she be able to tell if Samantha was lying?"

"That's true, you're probably right." I kept my eyes on his hand, still tracing circles on mine.

"Hey," he said. The fingers of his other hand brushed along my cheek. "We'll figure this out. Whatever it takes."

I tried to smile. "My head is all over the place."

"You know," he said, walking his fingers up my arm to rest on my shoulder. "I'm not trying to brag or anything, but I've been told I give a pretty decent hug."

I laughed. "Yeah? By who, your mom?"

He unfolded himself from the chair and placed his hand over his heart, shaking his head. "Ouch. That was a really low blow. Come on." He motioned for me to stand up and held his arms open for me.

I gripped the edge of the table and stared up at him for a moment. "You're serious?"

"I *never* joke about hugs." His arms were still wide open and he curved his fingers at me.

I drew in a deep breath and stood. Ethan reached out with both hands and smoothed the hair back from my face. Moving his hands down to my shoulders, he gently tugged me forward.

"It's okay," he said, wrapping his arms around me. He held me close as I inhaled his clean, warm scent. God, it felt good. I let myself go, burying my face in his shirt. My arms wound their way up around his back.

For several minutes, neither of us said anything. I felt a fissure crack down on the fortress of my emotions. Things I hadn't let myself really feel for so long -- fear, love, pain, all of it came rushing over me. There was something right about being here in his arms. I'd been so blinded by my sense of, what -- duty? Responsibility for my mother's condition? Whatever it was, I'd wasted years hardening my heart when I should have been letting someone inside. Someone like Ethan who was strong and patient and refused to give up on me.

I lifted my head and with one hand, reached up and placed my palm against his cheek. "Thank you. For not giving up on me, even when you should have."

He turned his head and kissed my palm. "I don't need magic powers to know you're the one for me." He shrugged. "I've always known."

It was crazy to feel happy when everything outside of the kitchen was so uncertain. But I reminded myself, I needed to let that go. There were things I could control and there were others I couldn't. Right then, where I stood, I couldn't do anything to change things. And just like that, the weight of all that guilt was lifted from my shoulders. I felt... good.

I smiled, really smiled at Ethan and he took a step back. "I better go. I have to work in the morning."

I stared up into his eyes, an urge to show him how I felt rose up inside me.

"Wait," I said, my heart rate picking up. He raised a brow. Placing my hands on his chest, I took a deep breath. I didn't have a lot of experience with this sort of thing, but it was time to be brave. I stood on my toes and kissed him, just a quick peck on the lips, but it was a big deal for me. As I pulled away, he reached for me. His eyes searched mine before he closed the distance between us. It started out gentle and sweet. He ran his hands up my neck and touched each side of my face. I lost myself in the softness of his mouth as the kiss deepened into something desperate and full of need.

I broke away, breathing hard. I could feel the color spread over my cheeks and when I looked up, Ethan smirked.

"I like it when you blush, I think it's cute," he said.

I laughed and shook my head. "You're incorrigible."

He grinned. "All part of my charm."

Smacking his chest, I pushed him toward the door. "Uh-huh."

Before he stepped out onto the porch, he turned toward me. "I'll give you a call tomorrow, okay?"

I nodded. "Sure." I waved as he strolled down the walk to his truck. But what I really wanted was to pull him back and kiss him until he was out of breath.

His taillights disappeared down the road and I went to shut the door when Niamh appeared and put a hand out to stop me. My heart dropped and I stared at her for a minute, unable to speak.

"I just need a minute," she said, glancing over her shoulder.

74

"Okay," I said, stepping aside so she could come in.

I love this house, it feels so welcoming.

I didn't say anything to that, just shook my head a little in surprise.

"When are you leaving?" I asked.

"That's actually what I wanted to talk to you about."

"All right," I said, sitting at the table.

Niamh sat across from me. "I think you should come to Tír na n'Óg with me."

"I can't go there," I said. "You know I have school and work. Plus my cousin's engagement party is next weekend."

"We have ways to get around that. I'll send decoys to cover for you. You don't have to worry," she waved her hand as though these things were irrelevant.

"Can the decoys teach me what I actually need to know for my career? Niamh, it's not that simple."

She sat at the table and leveled her gaze on me. "I know these things are important to you. But we need to find Aoife. We can't just wait for her to make her next move."

"You said yourself it could take months for her to prepare a binding spell."

"If that is in fact what she's doing. But either way I'd like to be one step ahead of her."

My whole life had led me to this point. Years of studying and working to save up so I could get into a decent graduate program and eventually earn a living to support my mother.

Niamh couldn't understand that. She didn't have to work and if she wanted something, she could just glamour a post-it note to look like a fifty dollar bill. If only I could do that.

"With enough practice, maybe you could," she said, and I shot her an annoyed look.

"Why do you think I should go, anyway?"

She crossed her legs and placed her hands on the table. "You're as much a part of this now as any of us. After what

Samantha told us, I feel it's important for us to stay together."

I wasn't sure how to respond. Calm, collected Niamh felt we should stay together?

You know, humans aren't the only ones affected when we spend time around each other.

What's that mean?

"Think about it. I've been spending so much time here, it's bound to change me on some level."

I hadn't really thought about it that way. I knew Liam and Aodhan had become more like the Danaan from being in Tír na n'Óg, so I guessed it made sense for it to work both ways.

"You won't become like Aengus, will you?" I asked, shuddering at the memory of Aoife's guard in Thunder Bay. Aengus had attacked Liam and I while we were trying to find Aodhan over the summer. Which reminded me, why wasn't Samantha's friend Ciarán like him? He was one of Aoife's people, shouldn't he be in the same emaciated state?

"No," Niamh said. "The only reason he was like that was from drawing magic from human blood. The iron in the blood goes directly into their bodies, poisoning them. As for your other question, Ciarán doesn't believe in what the others are doing. In fact, he's firmly against draining humans."

"That's a surprise. Why is he staying with them if he doesn't like what they're doing?"

"They told me he only stayed because Breanh had sealed the portal while Aoife was trapped in the fey globe. Then he met Samantha and I suppose he didn't want to stay away from her."

"Would she become delusional like my mother if he left?"

Niamh shook her head. "I'm not sure. I've never known any half-breeds in my lifetime."

"Anyway, even if it weren't for school…I can't miss Nicole's engagement party, she'd never forgive me."

"She'll never have to know. The sooner we figure out where Aoife is the sooner we can break the geis. I wouldn't ask if it weren't important. And I know Liam wouldn't dream of asking you."

"Why?" I asked, narrowing my eyes.

She shrugged. "He's in a very precarious position. He doesn't want to risk alienating you."

"I need some time to think about it," I said.

"Time is something we don't have. I'll give you until tomorrow," she said, her pale blue eyes burning into mine as she rose from her seat.

I nodded. "I understand. I just have a lot to figure out."

I blinked and she was gone, the door clicking shut the only sign of her departure.

Chapter Nine

"Come on Beth, we need to board," a girl with springy copper ringlets says, her voice pleading.

"One more minute, he might still show," a blonde says, turning as she looks around the crowded airport.

The redhead sighs, glancing among the swarming faces. "He would have been to see you by now. You're acting crazy."

The blonde is my mother. Her face is drawn, dark circles standing out under her green eyes. She bites her lip as the other girl tugs on her arm. Tears begin to fall as her shoulders slump.

"Come on, Bethy. You're too good for him anyway." The girl's eyes are darting toward the departure gate where a flight attendant is taking down the sign for Flight 407.

My mother's eyes drop to the floor and she allows the girl to tug her forward. As the redhead speaks to the flight attendant, my mother glances over her shoulder one last time before they run down the boarding ramp.

Sunlight peeked through my blinds and I rolled over to bury my head into my pillow. My head was pounding and my mouth was dry and cottony. I'd spent most of the night wide awake, only the moonbeams keeping me company. The last time I'd checked the clock, it was quarter to five. It was now almost eight and I had a class at ten.

I'd gone back and forth all night on what I would tell

Niamh today. I looked at the corkboard hanging over my desk. A few awards and medals I'd won in high school hung around pictures of me and Nicole at different ages. One was us after a dance recital at six and seven years old, dressed in colorful costumes, our hair in tight curls. Another of us jumping off the diving board of her pool together at eleven and twelve.

Nicole's engagement party itself wasn't what was important to me. It was being there for her that mattered. She'd probably never know it wasn't me if a decoy took my place. Not only would whoever Niamh sent be glamoured to look like me, but the entire party would be compelled to believe it was me, no matter how I behaved. It was what came after — the guilt. I'd never forget I wasn't there and I hated the thought living with that feeling.

The memory of my mother's face from my dream flashed in my mind. Her heartbreak and pain at feeling abandoned in every glance.

The difference between my mother's situation and Nicole's were astronomical. Maybe the truth was that I was afraid of going back *there*, to Tír na n'Óg. Back to the place where everything felt wrong and perfect at the same time. In Tír na n'Óg the sun always shone, the air was clean and none of Earth's rules applied. It was all beautiful women and breathtaking men, dancing and feasting and, of course, plenty of seduction. Even the way the clothing felt on my skin was alluring.

If Nicole knew the truth, she would tell me to go after Aoife. I knew that much for sure. The university would possibly grant me a leave of absence, especially if one of Niamh's people was asking for it in my place.

I climbed out of bed and sat down at my desk to turn on the computer. I typed up an email to my professor, telling him I had a family emergency and I'd be out class for at least today. My finger twitched over my mouse as I debated whether to click send or not.

I pressed send and closed my eyes. There was an application for a leave of absence on the university's website. Shaking my head, I filled it out. There was a chance I could get thrown out of the graduate program for this. But I didn't want a decoy taking my classes for me, it didn't sit well. I drew up the image of my mother in Tír na n'Óg when she'd been completely normal. Her smile when she spoke to me and Liam was all the incentive I needed to send it off and shut down my computer.

I changed into some jeans and a T-shirt before heading downstairs. I felt lighter than I had in weeks. We were finally going to take steps toward making things as they should be between my parents. We would find Aoife, and this time I would destroy the amulet she wore and break the geis that kept my parents apart.

Everyone was doing their normal Monday morning thing in the kitchen. Gram was at the stove fussing over scrambled eggs. Pop sat at the table reading the newspaper. My mother sat beside him slowly spreading butter on a piece of toast.

"Something smells amazing," I said as I kissed the top of my mother's head.

I looked at the two empty chairs. The same chairs Ethan and I had sat in just last night. I could be honest with him and tell him what we were up to this time. I knew he'd understand why I had to miss the party. Grabbing my phone off the sideboard, I sent him a quick text letting him know I needed to talk.

"There's plenty here, just grab a plate sweetheart," Gram said without turning around.

"First things first," I said as I went over to the coffee pot.

After I added my cream and sugar I went to the stove and kissed her on the cheek. "Love you Gram."

She looked up from the stove and smiled at me. "Well, I love you too, Allie-girl."

"How about one of those smooches for the old man?" Pop said, looking at me from over his reading glasses.

"Of course," I said as I pulled a plate down for myself. I walked over and planted a loud one right on his balding head. "You're the best, Pop."

My mother just watched me as she nibbled her toast. I gave her a tiny smile. Big gestures tended to set her off.

My phone beeped.

I'm ten minutes away. Be right over.

"Feeling sentimental today, are you?" Pop asked, his face buried in the newspaper again.

I shrugged. "Not really, just thinking you guys are pretty darn awesome. But I think that every day."

"Uh-huh, we are *pretty awesome,*" Gram said, eyes twinkling as she carried the pan of eggs to the table. "Well, whatever it is, I'll take it."

I attempted to push down what-if thoughts as I ate my breakfast. What if I could never come back? What if something happened with my mother while I was gone? What if I failed completely and Liam became bound to Aoife forever? If I kept that line of thinking, I'd never leave.

Just then there was a knock at the back door. I looked over into the living room and saw Liam and Niamh standing outside.

"Oh, come on in you two," Gram hollered.

They walked in and my eyes widened as I took in Niamh's outfit. They were both in track pants and T-shirts.

"Good morning, everyone," Liam said. "Sorry to interrupt breakfast, but we were going for a run and wondered if Allison would like to join us?"

I heard your decision, Allison.

So you thought that meant we should go for a run?

The sooner we leave, the better.

I looked at the faces seated around the kitchen table, a knot forming in my throat. They'd be fine. Ethan would make sure everything was okay while I was gone.

Liam cleared his throat and I jerked up. "Yeah, a run sounds good." Normally I liked to get my run in before I had breakfast, so I crossed my fingers that my grandparents didn't notice.

I stood and brought my half-eaten plate of eggs to the sink. Gram stood and grabbed the plate out of my hands. "Go on, I'll take care of these."

I swallowed. "Thanks Gram. I'll see you soon, okay?"

I said goodbye to my family and followed Liam and Niamh out the back door, unsure when I'd see them all again.

Once we were off the back porch I turned to Niamh.
So, this is it?

We just need to go to Liam's house to take care of one thing and we'll head to Wheelwright.

I followed them next door. From the bottom of the driveway, I saw Samantha and Ciarán sitting on Liam's front stoop, staring at each other. Samantha's chin jutted out and I could tell they were having a silent conversation.

"Are they coming?" I asked Niamh under my breath.

She answered me in my head. *Liam and I both came to get you so they could have a chance to talk. Ciarán doesn't think Samantha should go to Tír na n'Óg.*

"I take it she doesn't like that idea?" I whispered as Samantha threw her arms up and stalked a few yards away from him.

I thought about whether Samantha going with us would be a good idea. *What do you two think?*

We both think she should come, as long as she removes all the steel from her body.

Confused, I turned to look at Niamh. Then I realized what she meant. Samantha had dozens of piercings on her ears and face. And if they were steel, they were made from iron.

"Good morning," I said to Samantha, glancing over to where Ciarán sat scowling off into the distance.

"Hey," she said, wiggling her fingers at me. On her hands were black fingerless gloves. She was wearing a crocheted black sweater over a black tank top and tight jeans. I glanced down at my faded jeans and T-shirt. She was so different from me. It was hard to believe we were related.

Samantha's eyes darted behind me to Niamh. She shook her head and looked at Ciarán. In a flash he was beside us. I didn't even see him move.

He looked at me, his eyes wide. "I don't think Sam should go with you. She's got a life here, a job. I agreed when I thought she was just coming to warn you and Liam. But not this, I don't want her getting mixed up in this."

Samantha pushed him hard enough that he stepped back. "I'm already mixed up in this," she said. "Besides, what kind of life do I have? My parents think I'm crazy. They barely talk to me if they can help it. Maybe I can help somehow."

She met my eyes, and hers were so blue, so like Aoife's, but with one major difference. They were full of emotion.

"Allison?" I swung around to find Ethan walking up the driveway. "Your grandmother said you went for a run with Liam and I heard voices up here. What's up?" He glanced at the group gathered on Liam's front lawn.

A lump formed in my throat. "Hey," I said, rubbing my hands together. "We were just… making plans."

I turned to Liam. "I'm really thirsty. Is it okay if I grab some water inside?"

Liam gestured toward the house. "Of course."

"Come with me?" I said to Ethan. I wanted to tell him what was going on in private.

I led him into the foyer and shut the door behind him. He followed me to the dining room and when I sat, he took the seat beside me. He caught my eyes and raised his brows expectantly.

"Niamh asked me to go to Tír na n'Óg with her and Liam."

"What, you mean go right now?" Ethan asked.

I nodded. "She doesn't want to wait until Aoife makes a move. In a way I agree with her."

"Did you tell me you needed to talk so you could just tell me you were leaving?"

I glanced up at him. "Yes, I hoped you'd understand."

"No Allison. I don't understand," he said, jumping up so fast the chair nearly fell over.

I hesitated. "Niamh came by after you left last night. I know there's a lot going on here, but I've thought about it all night. The sooner we take care of the threat Aoife poses on all of us, the better."

Ethan stared at me, his face hard. "I understand that part. But I told you whatever happens, I'm coming with you."

"What?" I said, shaking my head. "You can't."

"Like hell I can't." He crossed his arms, eyes narrowed. "You're not leaving me behind this time."

He was angry, but the glint in his eyes shone with fear.

"If there was something dangerous you needed to do, would you do it without me?"

"Not if you asked me not to."

"There's no way for me to know how long we'll be gone. It could be a few hours, or weeks. I can't ask that of you."

"You don't have to ask. Wherever you go, I go."

With a sigh I relented, selfishly glad to not be leaving him behind.

"Okay," I said. "Niamh is going to send a decoy to cover for me, hopefully she can do the same for you."

When we went back outside, the air was still thick with tension. I looked at Niamh who stood beside Liam watching the internal ping-pong match between Samantha and Ciarán.

Ethan wants to come with us.

She nodded as if she knew, and she probably did.

I'm beginning to think we should just go on without these two.

Liam turned to me and Ethan. "You haven't heard anything from Aodhan right?"

"Not since Friday."

"All right," he said frowning. "I suppose I should leave him a note."

"Should I take my truck to wherever we're going?" Ethan asked.

Liam's brows rose. "You're coming?"

I sighed. "Yep, he doesn't want to be left behind."

"No, I think that's good," Liam said and I did a double-take.

"You do?"

"If Aodhan isn't coming this time, the more of us keeping an eye on you the better."

I scoffed. "You make me sound so *precious*."

Ethan nudged my side. "That's because you are," he said softly.

I shot him a look. "I didn't mean that in a good way. More like *pathetic*."

"Anyway, yes," Liam said. "You might as well take your truck. Leaving it on the street wouldn't be good."

"I don't know the way," I said. "At least not by regular roads."

"What's that supposed to mean?" Ethan said.

I rolled my eyes at how absurd it would sound. "They don't use cars. They don't need to."

"What she means is we travel faster on foot. We can get to Wheelwright in a few minutes if we run," Niamh said.

Ethan whistled low. "I know how to get to Wheelwright. Can you give me an address?"

Liam and Niamh explained how Ethan would have to go to get to the old house where the portal was hidden. It was tucked away on a wildlife sanctuary, far away from the iron and pollution of the cities and suburbs. It would be a miracle if Ethan's four wheel drive would make it up the overgrown cart road leading in, but Ethan was confident the truck could handle it.

With the rest of them going on foot, Ethan and I climbed into the truck alone. Ciarán would need to carry Samantha. Apparently that didn't bother her as much as it had bothered me. My stomach twisted at the memory of flying through the air in Liam's arms. He ran so fast I couldn't even open my eyes from the pressure. After that, I'd asked them to knock me out when we had to travel like that.

We didn't really talk for the first twenty minutes of the ride. Ethan called his father to tell him he wasn't feeling well and needed to take the rest of the day off. I stared out the window, trying to quiet the annoying voice that gnawed at me about the people and things I was leaving behind. It didn't matter that I thought I'd come to peace with my decision, the voice was not going anywhere.

"So tell me what it's like in this place we're going. *Teer Nah Nog*. My memory is pretty fuzzy," Ethan said, glancing over at me.

I took a deep breath. "It's incredibly beautiful there. Overwhelmingly beautiful. It takes a while to adjust to how different everything is. I can't really describe it, but maybe it could be compared to being on drugs. Like in movies when someone's on an acid trip, everything feels louder and brighter and just ... more."

"Groovy," Ethan said, and I could tell he was trying to lighten my mood.

"Something like that," I said. "Another thing is everything is *alive*. Maybe that's not the right word. Maybe sentient fits better. The plants and trees respond when you touch them, it's extraordinary. The houses are made from the trees. The trees that grow on the hillside form their roots into the frames of the houses. Then the Danaans add on to make homes. Niamh's house is this elaborate underground mansion. You have to see it to believe it."

"I sort of remember Aoife's place felt like a castle. In my memories, the walls were gray stone with tapestries hung from them."

I looked out the window at the passing trees as we got further into the country. "Aoife's house is in a cave. It's much different from Niamh's. And even more spectacular is the Bruidhean. That's where the king and queen live. It means fairy palace in English."

Ethan nodded, keeping his eyes on the road. "In one of my high school English classes we read this play about fairies. I can't remember what it's called, but Miss Bouchard got this weird, maniacal gleam in her eyes whenever she read parts of it out loud. Do you know what I'm talking about?"

I laughed, remembering the teacher he was talking about. She was an odd one. "Yes, it was *A Midsummer's Night Dream* by Shakespeare."

"The way you just described Tír na n'Óg reminded me of that."

I smacked his arm. "You think I'm weird and maniacal?"

"No, no. Not that part. Just like you were in a trance remembering."

"I know a bank where the wild thyme blows,
Where oxlips and the nodding violet grows,
Quite over-canopied with luscious woodbine,
With sweet musk-roses and with eglantine."

"Yeah, that's the one," Ethan said, slapping his steering wheel.

"You'll see. And I guarantee you'll have a maniacal gleam in your eyes when you're there."

He swiped my hand off the bench seat and gave it a quick kiss. "I look forward to it."

We got to the access road in about thirty minutes and bumped along for about a mile. It had been so long since a vehicle had been on this road that the indents from wheels were barely noticeable anymore. The trees rose on either side obstructing the blue sky with foliage. We saw our entire group waiting for us in a clearing, knee-high in grass. Ethan stopped the truck and we both jumped out.

"I think this is about as far in as you'll get," Liam said to Ethan. "There's a ditch up ahead that isn't worth the trouble. It's only about a half-mile more."

Ethan nodded and locked up his truck. Mosquitoes attacked us as we walked, creating a buzzing cloud around our heads. Luckily, it wasn't long until I could see the old farmhouse. It was a pale yellow colonial built hundreds of years ago, but Niamh and her people kept it so well-maintained it was in perfect condition. There were a few outbuildings and a barn, but I didn't know if they even used them. The most important part of the property was the root cellar behind the house that held the portal to Tír na n'Óg.

The front door opened and a tall, dark-haired figure stepped out. Diarmuid was Niamh's adviser. He assisted her in decision-making and guarded the portal in her absence. Trailing behind him was his mate, Eithne. She was a slight girl with fair skin and long cinnamon waves down her back.

Too fast for my eyes to pick up, they were in front of us. Eithne gave me a tentative smile before greeting Niamh and Liam. But when she looked at Niamh, her expression fell. I knew Niamh was telling her who Samantha was. Eithne had been the one to give me the first inkling that Aoife had a big secret she was keeping from Liam. I still didn't know exactly how or why, but I knew somehow Aoife had forced Eithne to hide Samantha in the human realm. And Eithne was terribly afraid of Aoife.

"Samantha, this is my adviser Diarmuid and his mate Eithne," Niamh said, her voice smooth.

Samantha gave a little finger wave, but didn't say anything. But Eithne stared at Samantha, her lips parted in wonder. As Eithne gaped, Samantha's expression was marked with confusion.

"What? Is something wrong?" Samantha asked,

glancing at Ciarán with wide eyes.

Niamh sighed. "Nothing's wrong. Come on. We can talk inside before we go."

Samantha gave Ciarán another perplexed look before they took off toward the front door of the house.

"Did I tell you Eithne was the one who had to find a place for Samantha after she was born?" I whispered to Ethan while we walked a few paces behind everyone else.

He laughed. "No, but I probably wouldn't have remembered who you were talking about anyway. These people have some weird names."

"True," I said, grinning at him. "I wish I had a cheat sheet most of the time, and I've met a lot of them already."

"Do you think Samantha and Ciarán are coming?" he asked, keeping his voice to a whisper.

I shrugged. "Beats me. I guess we just have to go along with whatever."

Eithne held the door open for us and I thanked her and asked if she remembered Ethan. She nodded and tilted her head in confusion when he held out a hand to her.

"I guess shaking hands is kind of a human thing," I said and Ethan quickly pulled his hand back.

"Oh, sorry. It's nice to meet you," he said, flashing her a sheepish grin.

"So nice to meet you, too, Ethan," she said and we all walked inside.

We joined everyone around the enormous round table that took up the entire dining room. There were just enough chairs for all eight of us.

Niamh stood. "Before we make further plans, I want to clear up some confusion," she said, glancing around the table.

"When you were born Samantha, Eithne was Aoife's handmaiden. Liam and Eithne were friends, allies even." She looked at Eithne, who had gone paler than usual.

"When Aoife found out she was carrying Liam's child,

she became irrationally jealous. She wanted Liam all to herself and was afraid a baby would steal all of his attention. So she hid in this realm during her pregnancy, keeping it a secret from all of us."

"That's just plain crazy," Samantha said. "Who gets jealous of a tiny baby?"

"That is the nature of her feelings for Liam," Niamh said, frowning.

Liam stared at his folded hands resting on the table top, jaw clenched.

"Anyway, Eithne was forced to find you someplace to live. She dropped you off at a hospital in Thunder Bay. The same hospital where your adoptive father works, Samantha."

Samantha's mouth dropped open. She glanced at Eithne and back to Niamh.

Eithne sucked in her lips. "I am so sorry. I didn't want to. But I had no choice." Her voice was barely a whisper. She looked at Liam, chewing on her lip again. But he didn't look at her.

Of all the Danaan I'd met, Eithne was the most like a human. She reminded me of a newborn foal, skittish and shy. It must have been horrible being Aoife's handmaiden, it was no wonder she was so nervous.

Diarmuid placed his hand on her shoulder. "Liam, Eithne tells the truth. Aoife forced her hand in this, both in commanding her to take Samantha away and keeping it a secret all this time."

"Samantha met Aoife in Thunder Bay after she escaped the fey globe. That's how Samantha found out about Allison and Liam," Niamh said to Eithne and Diarmuid as she sat down again.

Eithne's eyebrows rose and she turned to Samantha. "She told you about Liam?"

Samantha let out a breath. "She told me my father had another family and didn't want anything to do with either of us."

Liam's hands came down hard on the table, but Niamh cut him off. "That is just not true, Samantha."

"That's why I didn't want you to know I was there," she said, looking at me and stealing glances at Liam.

"Unbelievable," I said under my breath.

Liam cleared his throat. "Do you believe I didn't know, Samantha?" His voice was tight and his eyes were full of the same pain he held when he'd found out I was his daughter.

"Yeah," she said. "I do now."

"Why did Aoife even bother saying anything if she was just going to lie?" I asked.

"I'm wondering the same thing," Niamh said.

"We should discuss your plans from here on," Diarmuid said to Niamh.

"The first thing we need to know is if Samantha and Ciarán are coming with us," Niamh said, raising her eyebrows at them.

Samantha folded and unfolded her hands and I could hear the click of her lip-piercing hitting her teeth. She shrugged one shoulder. "I think I should go," she said, glancing at Ciarán from the corner of her eyes. "If you guys want me to, that is."

"You don't think she ought to go?" Diarmuid asked Ciarán, his thick eyebrows drawn in.

Ciarán shifted, placing both hands on the table. "No," he said, swallowing. "I'm not sure what Aoife has planned, but I don't want Sam to have any part of it."

"Not," she said, glaring at him "that it's your decision to make."

Ciarán pushed away from the table and jumped up, moving to the window in the blink of an eye. His back to the room, he said, "No, of course not."

"I think the real issue is whether you'll be able to stand up to Aoife when the time comes," I said, looking at Samantha.

She tore her eyes away from Ciarán's back. "You think

I'd throw you to the wolves?"

I held up my hands. "That's not what I'm saying. I'm just being realistic."

"Well, you're wrong."

"You shouldn't be in that position in the first place," Ciarán said, turning toward Samantha.

They continued to stare at each other, and as the seconds passed, I grew irritated.

Niamh stood and broke the silence. "While you two work that out, we will go on ahead."

Ciarán visibly relaxed and Samantha looked deflated. But Niamh's tone allowed no argument.

Liam watched Niamh, his lips forming a thin line. When his eyes narrowed, I figured they were discussing her decision internally.

I pushed myself up, ready to leave this place. "All right, let's get this show on the road."

Ethan followed me toward the door. I turned and looked at Samantha. She hung her head and scowled at the chipped polish on her fingernails.

"I'll see you soon, Samantha," I said, hoping to catch her eye before I left.

When her gaze slid over to me, her cheeks were flushed with anger. She nodded and quickly averted her eyes.

I hurried out the front door, Ethan in my wake. I spun around and widened my eyes. "Those two are going to strangle each other," I said quietly.

"No kidding," he said. "I was waiting for Ciarán to burst into flames from the looks she kept giving him."

"You're sure you want to do this?" I said. "It's not too late to change your mind."

Ethan leaned toward me as we walked around back. "I haven't changed my mind. Stop hoping I will."

"Just checking," I said.

The front door slammed shut. Niamh and Liam appeared next to us.

Liam didn't say anything, but his hands were clenched at his sides. I was betting seeing Samantha and Ciarán argue bothered him. It was hard for me not to tell them to cut it out, too.

"Diarmuid is going to have an earful for me next time I see him," Niamh said with a laugh.

Ethan and I just looked at each other and I shrugged.

"I left him with Samantha and Ciarán. He'll never let me forget it."

I laughed out loud at that. "They do antagonize each other."

Liam gave me a bland look, so I dropped it.

Niamh stopped at the battered wooden door built into the hillside leading down to the root cellar. She waved her hand over the rusty lock and I heard a click. I'd heard the Danaan could use their minds to manipulate objects, but this was the first time I'd seen it in action.

Niamh glanced over her shoulder at me and smirked. Waving her fingers again, the door creaked open.

Show off.

I could hear her chuckle as she went down the steps.

Jealous.

Ethan gestured for me to follow Liam through the doorway. I stepped over the threshold onto the stairs. Several were cracked and loose and I made my way down carefully.

The door closed with a thud behind me and I heard Ethan's steps coming down. The root cellar was a cool, musty stone chamber that reminded me of a burial crypt. Canning jars filled the shelves lining two of the walls.

Niamh put her hand on the far wall and a warm glow worked its way up her arm and filled the room. My eyelids fluttered shut against the intensity of the light. I forgot myself in that moment until I felt a hand at my waist gently pushing me forward.

I held my arms up to shield my eyes and took a few tentative steps toward the light. When the brightness faded, I opened my eyes. Everything seemed to slow down. Voices bounced and echoed in my head.

Chapter Ten

When my eyes focused, I saw I was in the familiar dining room in Niamh's house in Tír na n'Óg. An enormous wooden table took up most of the room. White walls arched up around us, framed by thick roots growing to the floor.

I stumbled to the first chair and collapsed onto it. Ethan did the same beside me. I squeezed my eyes shut to wait out the vertigo assaulting my senses.

Once the feeling had ebbed, I glanced around the room. Ethan turned his head toward me. His eyes were wide and he shook his head.

"That was pretty intense," he said as his fingers found mine.

I laughed under my breath. "You could say that."

"How are you feeling?" Liam asked, leaning on the table beside me.

I swallowed. "I feel better than last time." Maybe knowing what to expect made it a little easier to accept the loss of equilibrium.

"That's good. How about you Ethan?"

"Honestly, I feel like I have a pretty good buzz," Ethan said.

"That's completely normal," Niamh said from across the table.

"Just give us a minute and we can go talk to Saoirse," I said, rubbing a hand across my eyes.

"Of course," Niamh said. "I have a few things to take care of. Would you like to lie down for a while?"

I looked at Ethan who shook his head. "No, that's not necessary. I could use some water, though."

Leaving Ethan and Liam at the table, Niamh led me down a hall and up a winding staircase. We passed the weapons room I'd stopped in with Aodhan on my last trip to Tír na n'Óg.

When I thought his name, Niamh's shoulders stiffened. She turned toward an arch and stopped, then stared at me for a moment like she was making a decision.

I haven't said this to anyone else. But Aodhan's absence from this journey has me worried.

She walked into the archway without waiting for me to respond. It led down a long, narrow stone passage. I heard the gurgling sound of water as we walked around a wide corner. At the end, the passageway opened into a cavern. I sucked in a breath. On one side, an underground stream bubbled past. From somewhere above, natural light poured in, casting the water a sparkling turquoise. Rocks formed a smooth ridge above the river that looked like the perfect place to sit and dip your feet in. And I was so entranced by it, I almost did.

Niamh stopped, gesturing for me to wait. I shook my head to clear it. The beauty of this place had put me under a spell.

This is where we bathe. The falls are up the river. Grab a pitcher and we'll get some fresh water for everyone to drink.

What do you think is going on with Aodhan?

She took a deep breath and met my eyes.

I don't know. But he was committed to making things right for you and your mother. Something is keeping him, but I haven't any idea what it is.

I was sure Aodhan had gained several enemies over the years. His entire life was spent protecting humans from

Danaans. My mind went to Aengus. When we were in Thunder Bay, Aodhan had put him into submission and ordered Niamh's guards to "take care of him." I assumed that meant kill him, but I never asked.

Could Aengus be alive and had he tracked Aodhan down to Liam's house?

Aengus is dead.

Niamh answered so confidently, I knew she was certain.

But what about the others? Beside Aengus and Ciarán, weren't there more of Aoife's guards in Thunder Bay?

Yes, two others. I wish we saw Aodhan before we left. Something feels wrong about him not being here with you.

She led me up a narrow, snaking lip between the stream and the cavern wall. Dappled light came from high above in what appeared to be naturally formed skylights. The echoing roar of a waterfall became louder each step we took.

I think he's done more than enough for me. More than I ever hoped for. I wouldn't blame him if he just wanted a little break.

As we rounded the next bend, the entire cavern opened to the sky about thirty feet up. The water poured from the top of one of the moss-covered walls into a clear pool.

Niamh held out her hand and I gave her the pitcher I carried in. It floated just above her hands and she stared at it as it flew across the pool and filled with water from the falls. With a tiny flick of her wrist the pitcher returned to hover in front of me.

"I try not to do things like that when we're in your world. But since we're here, I don't have any reason to hide what I really am."

I reached out and grabbed the pitcher and cradled it in my arms.

"That must be strange," I said. "To have to hide so many things. Wouldn't you be happier if you could just seal the portals and leave our world behind forever?"

"Yes and no," Niamh said, as we picked our way back

toward the heart of the cavern.

"What if Aodhan came back here with you?" I asked, surprised at my boldness.

"Before I met you, that was all I dreamed of."

"Do you think you two will ever work things out?"

Her smile was sad. "I've been hoping he would forgive me for a long time. I haven't given up, but I don't see it happening any time soon."

We walked up the stone steps back into the main part of Niamh's house. She pointed down the hall past the weapons room. "Just down there are the guest quarters. If you'd like, you may stay here this evening."

Back down in the dining room Ethan was laughing at something Liam said. Watching the two of them was like looking at a couple of old friends. It was completely surreal.

Niamh closed her eyes and some drinking cups floated into the room and landed on the table. Ethan's eyes widened and he slid me a questioning look.

"Oh, didn't I mention the telekinesis?" I said, laughing. "Up until today I've only seen it a couple times."

"That's pretty cool. Can you do that Liam?"

Instead of answering, Liam focused on the pitcher full of water. Nothing happened at first, but after a minute, it levitated and tipped enough to fill one of the cups before setting back down.

"Whoa, nice," Ethan said, clapping Liam on the back.

The cool water helped clear my head and I was ready for the next move. We would walk to the Bruidhean to talk to Saoirse. Like Deaghlan, Saoirse didn't even try to mask her otherness. She was incredibly beautiful and just looking at her was like staring into the sun.

She was too alluring, too much for one person to take in.

That first step outside in Tír na n'Óg felt like walking into a fairytale. I don't think words can describe the way everything comes to life before your eyes. It's like being legally blind your entire life and then you put on super strength glasses and everything comes into Technicolor focus.

Niamh and Liam walked ahead of us, and I could tell it was difficult for them to keep our slow human pace.

Ethan reached over and grasped my hand. I looked up at his face and he was grinning like he was punch-drunk. I choked on my laugh.

"What?" he asked.

"Nothing," I said. "I just recognize that look on your face."

"Yeah?" he asked, tipping his head to the side. "What look would that be?"

I shrugged. "You look like I felt the first time I was here. Overwhelmed, awestruck."

"Uh-huh," he said, yanking me closer as we walked. "Don't forget this is my second time here."

I peeked at him, knowing he was teasing me. "So none of this affects you this time?"

He lowered his head and whispered in my ear. "Some things always affect me."

"Hmm," I said blushing. He was still just as cocky in this world as any other.

Bright light filtered through countless trees surrounding the path to the Bruidhean. I smoothed my hair back with my free hand as we walked.

"Wait!" I turned around just as Samantha ran up to us. Her eyes were wide and she wrapped her arms around her sides.

"I thought of something else I needed to tell you," she said as Niamh and Liam walked back to us.

My brows rose. "Okay."

"Aoife had this necklace she kept rubbing between her fingers while she talked to the others. She said it wasn't enough, but she knew where to find more. Something about a falling mine?"

Niamh's eyes narrowed as she listened to Samantha.

"Not falling mines. Fháillan mines. But no more fháillan mines are left in Tír na n'Óg."

"I'm sorry," Samantha said, fidgeting. "That's all I remember. But it seemed important."

"Where's Ciarán?" Liam asked.

Samantha looked down at the ground, wringing her hands. "I left him back at the house. He wouldn't agree I should come, but I *needed* to."

I looked at Ethan, who just shrugged. "Does that mean he'll be right behind you?" I asked.

"I don't think so. They were all sleeping when I left."

"I'm glad to see you've removed the steel from your body. Is it all gone?" Niamh asked.

"Uh, yeah. Ciarán and I had a talk about that. I honestly had no idea. I don't know why he never told me that iron was like kryptonite to all of you."

I started to ask her how she got through the portal, but she beat me to it.

"I looked in your thoughts while you were going. I saw Niamh put her hand up on the wall in the root cellar, so that's what I did."

Niamh looked uneasy, but Liam looked impressed. I didn't know what to think.

"We're on our way to see my mother," Niamh said as she started walking. Samantha hesitated. Niamh glanced over her shoulder. "Come along."

Samantha looked so relieved I thought she'd burst. She scampered over to my side and gave me a tentative smile.

"It's really cool here," she said, a grin peeking through.

"It's incredible," I said, looking at her. She was at least two inches shorter than me. I realized I didn't even know how old she was.

"Twenty-three," she said, walking along.

I rolled my eyes at Ethan and laughed. "It was bad enough having Niamh answer my thoughts out loud, now I have you doing it too."

Samantha's hand flew up to her mouth, eyes wide. "Sorry about that," she said. "I've really gotten a lot better at not doing it, I swear."

"I was just teasing. So, you're twenty-three and so am I. That's pretty weird. For sisters."

"Yeah, I guess. I'll be twenty-four next month, so we're almost a year apart," she said.

"How did you know how old I am?" I asked.

"Oh, when you were telling me how old you were, you were thinking about your birthday and how it's in June," she said, shrugging as though this happened all the time.

"It *does* happen all the time," she said, giving me an apologetic glance. "I mean, I don't really have many friends. People are always weirded out by me. My parents can't even stand being in the same room as me. So, yeah I try not to answer thoughts out loud, but it doesn't always work."

My heart did a little flip-flop. Aside from the whole answering people's unspoken questions, I could totally relate to what she'd just said. It might have been for different reasons, but my whole life most people never felt comfortable around me. A lot of that had to do with not knowing what to say to the daughter of a schizophrenic. But it had been a while since I'd let it bother me.

Ethan was quiet as we walked. I glanced at him and he was transfixed looking at the flowers and trees, taking it all in. I did feel much more lucid during this trip to Tír na n'Óg. Samantha seemed to be fine, too. I assumed it was her Danaan blood that kept her from being affected.

Without turning around, Niamh said, "That's right, Allison. You have some too, which makes the transition between worlds a little easier."

"Have some what?" Ethan said, looking at me with a lopsided grin.

"Danaan blood," I said. He might not admit it, but I could tell he was feeling it. His eyes were just a little shinier than usual and his smile was just a little goofier. "I was thinking about Samantha being part Danaan and that's why she isn't overwhelmed by the differences here."

No matter what my frame of mind was, Tír na n'Óg was magnificent. I took in the cornflower blue sky. Here, it only rained at night. Fluffy white clouds had just started floating in overhead, which told me it was late afternoon.

We reached the top of a hill, which held a spectacular view of a river valley below. Just beyond that river, a mountain range stretched up and along as far as the eye could see. Within the tallest mountain lay the Bruidhean. Hundreds of Danaan lived in its walls. At the heart of the palace was where the king and queen lived.

"Whoa," Samantha said as we made our way down toward the river. "It's like we're stepping onto the set of *The Fellowship of the Ring*."

"That's funny. I thought the same thing the first time I saw it. Those movies were fantastic, but of course the books were better."

Samantha looked horrified. "You actually read all of those?"

I was going to defend my love of all things Tolkien, but Ethan spoke up. "Are you trying to get yourself killed? You can't tease Allison about books or you'll get the Look of Death."

My eyes narrowed, and for a minute I considered pushing him into the river. But instead, I had to laugh. "Hey, say whatever you want. I'm a proud book nerd."

Samantha laughed too. "Books aren't really my thing," she said, and quickly added, "no offense."

"None taken," I said, shrugging. "It's fine. Different strokes and whatever."

The smile Samantha gave me was shy. "I'm more of a visual person. Painting, photography. I would love to shoot this place with a camera," she said, looking around.

Several yards up the river, an outcropping of large, flat

stones extended from one side of the river to the other, forming a natural bridge. Waterfowl in otherworldly shades of indigo and chartreuse dotted the pools around the stones. They watched as we crossed the river, bowing their slender necks, it seemed, in greeting.

"This must be what Snow White felt like," Samantha said under her breath as she hopped from stone to stone.

I laughed. "Just wait 'til you see the squirrels."

She whipped around, her eyes huge.

"I'm just kidding," I said, pressing my lips together to keep from laughing.

She studied me for a second before moving forward.

From the river, a stone path led to the base of the mountain. It eventually became a staircase that wove its way up through the trees to the entrance of the Bruidhean. The sky was darkening and small spheres of light, known as fey lights dotted the path.

Niamh led us into the large entryway. The heavy wooden door closing behind us echoed in the empty hall.

"Strange that I can't hear anyone," Niamh said, frowning.

"Very strange," Liam agreed.

I moved in closer to Ethan as we walked further inside. Just being here brought on a wide range of emotions. I'd seen my mother in this gathering room, sane and as clear headed as anyone. I'd been as helpless as a newborn foal when I met both Saoirse and Deaghlan. I'd also learned about the horrible things Breanh was doing to Ethan. I pushed back those memories, trying to keep my head clear for what lay ahead.

Nobody came out to greet us, the place felt totally deserted. Niamh moved faster, holding up a hand, telling us to wait. Her form blurred as she darted off to search for signs of anyone.

When she returned, her face was drawn tight. "My parents aren't here. Folk are about doing their regular activities. But my mother has gone to the shore to see the damage done to Aoife's land."

"Saoirse never leaves the Bruidhean," Liam said, frowning.

"There's more," Niamh said. "Aodhan's been here. He showed up this morning demanding to meet with the king and queen."

"What does that mean?" I asked. "Why didn't he tell us he was coming?"

Liam and Niamh stared at each other, their faces not giving anything away. I looked at Samantha.

Can you hear what they're saying to each other?

Her eyes flicked up to mine and she shook her head.

No. I can't get through their mind shields. It's really frustrating.

Niamh began pacing. "When Aodhan left Liam's house, he was livid. We just figured he needed some time to cool down after his falling out with my father."

"This is good though," I said. "Weren't we all wondering when your parents would do something about Aoife?"

"I suppose you're right," Niamh said, still pacing.

"What's the best thing to do now?" Liam said.

"We're going to Aoife's house, aren't we?" I said, looking between them.

"Of course," Niamh said. She took a deep breath and met my eyes.

Slow, deliberate footsteps came from the front entry. We all turned toward the gathering room entrance.

Deaghlan stood in the doorway, a slow smile slipping onto his face.

"And now you're here," he said, his arms held wide.

"Father," Niamh said, her brows furrowed.

"Your hero has come rushing in to save the day," Deaghlan said with a flourish of his hands.

Niamh tilted her head to the side, but didn't respond.

"After I came back to see about setting things right, Aodhan showed up and whisked your mother away to see for herself the damage Aoife has done," Deaghlan said, articulating each word.

"As though Mother didn't already know?" Niamh said, her brows shooting up.

"Of course she already knew. She knows all, doesn't she?"

Niamh didn't respond. Her face was a mask. I could almost see the cracks beginning to form as her all-too-human emotions fought to break free.

"Well, what are they doing about it? I asked Deaghlan.

He turned to regard me, much like someone would regard gum on the bottom of their shoe. I could tell the instant he noticed Samantha by my side.

Ignoring my question, he glided over to us. Samantha took a step back so she was behind me.

"What do we have here?" Deaghlan asked, his voice loaded with charm.

"This is Samantha," Liam said moving over to my other side.

"Well, hello Samantha," Deaghlan said, tilting his head to the side.

Samantha's voice was barely a whisper. "Hi."

"And this is Deaghlan, Niamh and Aoife's father," Liam said.

So that means he's my grandfather?

I busted out laughing and even Niamh smiled, hearing the question in Samantha's mind.

"That's correct, Samantha. He is your grandfather," Niamh said, barely concealing the laughter in her voice.

Deaghlan's reaction was priceless. His eyes bulged and his mouth gaped. He looked like a fish on the line.

"While this is all very entertaining, perhaps someone could explain to me what is going on?" Deaghlan said.

"The quick version is Aoife had a baby and didn't tell anyone. That's pretty much all you need to know," I said.

The line of Deaghlan's jaw tightened. "So it would

seem. Funny how Saoirse didn't see this coming."

Nobody spoke for a beat. I was never able to handle awkward silences well.

"If Aodhan and Saoirse are there, why aren't you with them?" I asked.

Surprise widened Deaghlan's eyes. "You're rather feisty, Allison. I like it."

I laughed without feeling. "You didn't answer the question."

In the blink of an eye, he was in front of me. "That's simple. Saoirse and Aodhan had things under control. I don't think my presence was required."

Ethan moved to my side, putting his hand on the small of my back. Deaghlan was completely unmoved.

My hands balled into fists. "What? Are you feeling left out, Deaghlan?"

Deaghlan prowled even closer, lowering his head so I could feel his warm breath. "Easy, Allison. You forget who you're talking to."

"Father, let's get back to the issue at hand," Niamh said.

He's right, Allison. Don't push him.

Staring at the floor, I pushed down the irritation inside me. Being mad at Deaghlan made it easier to not become ensnared by him. When I looked back up into his icy blue eyes, my anger was replaced with pure, raw fear.

Deaghlan smirked and stepped back. Without looking away, he said to Niamh, "Your mother won't be long. She'll return and you can make your plans. Perhaps even let me know what they are."

He turned on his heel and was gone.

"What is his deal?" I asked Niamh.

She sighed. "It's like you said. He's feeling left out. It happens whenever he neglects his responsibilities for too long and my mother makes decisions without him."

"I don't like the guy," Ethan said, his hand curving around my waist.

"Can't say I blame you," Liam said. "But don't do what Allison has done and provoke him."

I shrugged at the look he gave me. "Why should I let him bully me?"

"It's best to just let him go on and not react," Niamh said.

"Let's go find Aodhan and Saoirse," I said. "It's too bad you guys don't have phones in this place."

"I don't usually need one," Niamh said, smirking. "It must be the pollution in Aoife's land that's keeping me from reaching my mother. I've never come home and not been able to communicate with her."

"You've never had trouble hearing my thoughts around iron, how come that happens here?" I asked.

Niamh smiled. "*Here* is very different from *there*."

"Allison, I think it would be best if the three of you stay here and let Niamh and I go on ahead," Liam said.

I blinked. "No. No way," I said, not sure I heard him right.

"Let's not make this an argument," Niamh said. "It will take Liam and me minutes to get there, where it would take the entire group hours."

"Wait," I said, backing up. "What are we supposed to do here?

"Just wait. Get some rest if you can," Liam said.

I looked at Ethan to back me up, but the apologetic look he gave me said that wouldn't happen. Was I being irrational? Samantha's voice snuck into my head.

They'll be fast. It makes sense for them to go on ahead. Don't take it personally.

I blew out a breath. "Fine," I said, shrugging. "Go then."

Liam looked torn for a moment. "I'd like for you to trust me, okay?" he asked, looking between me and Samantha.

I didn't answer, but Samantha nodded. Liam ran his hands through his hair and with one last look, he and Niamh took off to find Aodhan and Saoirse.

Chapter Eleven

Within seconds of Niamh and Liam's departure, three young women came into the gathering room. They all wore jewel-toned gowns like most Danaan females. Their hair was braided with flowers and flowed down their backs.

The women led us upstairs and down several long hallways to what I remembered as the guest quarters. There was a common room in the center of a half-dozen bedrooms. Couches with throw pillows arranged haphazardly took up most of the space.

I fell back onto one of the plush cushions and rubbed the heel of my hand over my forehead. Now that I thought about it, I was exhausted.

"I'm tired too," Samantha said. "Does it matter which room I take?"

"I doubt it," I said, stretching my arms up behind my head.

"Okay, well wake me up if anything happens, I guess."

Ethan stood off to the side with his hands in the pockets of his jeans. He hadn't cut his hair in a while and when he looked down, a dark curl nearly touched his cheek. He smiled at me and my chest swelled.

"Don't you want to get some rest?" he asked.

"I guess so," I said, suddenly feeling awkward. "How are you feeling?"

He didn't answer right away. His gaze lifted to the high

arched ceiling before meeting mine. The corners of his eyes crinkled. "This might sound ridiculous. But I feel kind of like a piece of taffy that's been pulled and stretched and put back together."

I laughed. "Nope, not ridiculous. I actually know exactly what you mean."

He rubbed his hands together, his brow wrinkling. "I know this is going to sound wrong, but will you stay with me? I'm not coming on to you. I'd just feel better if you were with me."

"Yeah, no problem," I said, my voice coming out choked. I cleared my throat and tried again. "Let's go."

I stood and led him into the room I'd stayed in last time I was here. It was small, but comfortable. I sat on the edge of the bed and scooted over to make room for him.

I took off my shoes and crawled over to the other side of the bed. After getting under the covers, I positioned myself on my side so he had plenty of room.

Ethan slid under the blankets and stared up at the ceiling. Neither of us said a word for a minute.

Butterflies fluttered in my chest when he rolled onto his side to look at me. I wondered how many times he'd lain in bed with other girls and the thought pierced my heart.

"What's wrong?" he asked, concern etched in his forehead.

I was immediately grateful that Ethan couldn't read minds. A laugh bubbled out. "Nothing. I mean, I'm fine."

His eyes twinkled. "Are you nervous?"

I frowned. "What, you can hear my thoughts now, too?"

"Hey," he said, reaching over to smooth back my hair. "It's just me. I promise I'll behave."

I swallowed. Was he serious — *just him?*

He kept his hand on my cheek and whispered my name. Closing my eyes, I felt his touch all the way down to my toes. When I opened them again, he was still staring at me.

I looked down at his mouth and his lips spread into a

crooked smile. My eyes lifted to his and in a moment of bold-ness I said, "What if I don't want you to?"

His eyes widened, but he didn't hesitate. His hand slid down my arm to my waist. My pulse pounded when he pulled me closer. His lips brushed against mine, softly at first.

I raised my hand to the soft skin just above his elbow, shivering as his biceps tightened under my touch.

The kiss deepened and the world fell out from under me. In that moment, I forgot about the Danaans and everything that went along with them.

Ethan trailed kisses across my cheek, down my neck and a soft moan escaped me. I wasn't embarrassed, though. I wanted more, so much more. I yanked his shirt loose from his jeans and slid my hand up the contours of his back.

In one swift movement, I was on my back as he hovered over me. His arms were on either side of my head and his hands gently cupped my face. Bringing his lips down to mine again, he kissed me until we were both breathless.

Both of my hands slid up the back of his shirt and I pulled him to me, wanting him closer. But he pulled back, his breath ragged.

"You need to get some rest," he said, pressing his lips against my forehead. He put all his weight on one arm and trailed the tips of his fingers over my cheek and down my neck, resting his hand on my heart. I was sure he could feel it thundering in my chest.

I was about to protest when he placed one last kiss on my lips. He lifted himself off me and settled onto his side. My eyes drifted closed as he draped his arm across my stom-ach. I snuggled in closer, and he snaked his arm under my head. After burying my face into his T-shirt I willed my heart to slow down. Eventually I drifted off to sleep thinking about gentle breezes and warm sunlight.

I woke up in Ethan's arms. Without windows, I had no concept of how long I'd been asleep. I watched his chest rise and fall for a moment as he slept. A strange tickling sensation appeared in my head. It was Niamh's voice in my mind.

Good, I'm glad you're awake.

They were back. I sat up, disentangling myself from Ethan, debating whether to wake him or not. As soon as the thought crossed my mind, he shifted and opened his eyes.

"Morning," he said, the sound of sleep thick in his voice.

"Good morning," I said and looked away before he could see the blush creep up my neck.

"You going somewhere?"

"I was just about to wake you. Niamh and Liam are back."

Ethan sat up beside me and stretched. "Oh, that's good news."

"Yeah. We'd better go see what they have to say." I still hadn't met his eyes even though I knew I was being ridiculous. But I'd never slept in the same bed as anyone outside my family before, never mind a guy like Ethan.

"Hold on, Al. We're not gonna start this again, are we?" he said, putting his finger under my chin to turn my head to face him. I closed my eyes, trying to pull away.

"Look at me," he said, his voice only a whisper.

I exhaled and opened my eyes. He studied my face. "Are we good?"

I nodded, raising a hand to my neck. "Yeah, of course."

"Good, I thought I lost you there for a minute." He tried to laugh, but it came out strangled.

Guilt twisted my insides. I dug deep for the strength to be brave. Taking a breath, I leaned forward and gently pressed my lips against his.

When he pulled back, his grin was lopsided. "Much

better."

"Come on," I said with a smile. "Let's go before they send a search party for *us*."

Samantha was pacing in the common room when we walked in. She was tugging on the short strands of hair that framed her face. When she heard us enter, she pivoted around.

"They're back," I said, stopping a few feet in front of her.

She nodded and swallowed. "Niamh called up to me," she said, tapping on her temple. "She wants us to join them in the dining hall, I guess."

I turned toward the hallway I thought led to the stairs in time to see Niamh and Liam walk in.

"What happened?" I asked, filled with nervous energy.

Niamh and Liam exchanged a look. "My mother wants to be the one to tell you everything," Niamh said and gestured for us to follow.

I nodded and Ethan caught my hand as we started walking the way they'd come.

"You okay?" Ethan asked, threading his fingers through mine. "You look nervous."

"I'm okay." I shrugged. "I am a little nervous, I guess."

He squeezed my hand. "Don't be. You got this."

One look at his dimpled grin, and for a second I believed him. But then we walked into the dining hall and my stomach dropped.

Sitting at one end of the grand dining table was Saoirse. Her pale hands were folded on the tabletop. When she caught my gaze, she tipped her head to the side and smiled demurely.

Swallowing hard, I took the chair that Liam held out for

me. I couldn't tear my eyes away from Saoirse's opal eyes. Her gaze was as seductive as it was unnerving and a shiver passed through me.

Someone cleared their throat to my right and I blinked, the spell breaking. I looked over and Deaghlan was lounging in the chair at the opposite end of the table. His irritating smirk was in place as he unabashedly watched me.

Saoirse stood, her midnight blue gown flowing all around her. "Welcome, Allison. It's a pleasure to have you back with us."

Keeping my eyes on the embroidered pattern of her dress, I nodded. "Thank you," I said, focusing on the formalities.

"Ethan," Saoirse said in her honey-sweet voice. "I'm glad to see you've recovered from your difficulties from our last meeting."

While Niamh introduced Samantha to Saoirse, Ethan made the mistake of meeting her eyes. I nudged him under the table, but he just stared. I sucked in my bottom lip and tried not to laugh. I reached down and pinched his thigh, hard. He yelped and spun in his chair to look at me.

"Sorry," I whispered, making a face. "You were staring."

His eyes widened and he shook his head.

"It helps if you don't look in her eyes," I said under my breath.

He clasped his hands in his lap and stared down for a second.

I touched his arm. "Happens to me, too," I said.

On my other side, Samantha was still fidgeting with the edges of her hair, no doubt uncomfortable from the two immortal grandparents on either end of the table.

One of Saoirse's serving women piled fruit onto a platter in front of us. Another placed a tray of tiny cakes on the table. Both looked delicious and my mouth watered.

"So, I'd like to tell you about what's happened while

you've been away," Saoirse said. She held out a chalice and one of the women filled it.

Deaghlan shifted in his seat, and the insolent look he gave Saoirse made it obvious how unhappy he was.

Saoirse ignored him. "Yesterday, Aodhan came to see me," she said before taking a sip from her cup.

As I filled my plate with fruit and some of the little cakes I watched Niamh, but her expression didn't falter. She and Liam remained silent across the table from us.

"He didn't come alone. He had two of Aoife's guards held captive, and two of Niamh's guards came voluntarily. To say Aodhan was displeased would be putting it mildly," Saoirse said.

My eyes widened and Samantha sucked in a breath beside me.

"Can we get to the point?" Deaghlan said, drumming his fingers impatiently.

Saoirse ignored him. "Aodhan has offered to help revive Aoife's land."

"Which is *completely* unnecessary," Deaghlan said.

Without even a glance at Deaghlan, Saoirse continued. "He offered his assistance, but he had conditions. He'd like at least three of the four portals between our worlds sealed."

"Ridiculous," Deaghlan said.

I watched Saoirse put her lips to her cup and look at him, unaffected. I didn't understand their relationship. Niamh's lips quirked.

She tolerates him far better than anyone else.

"What about Aoife? Do you know where she is?" I asked.

"Aoife was not there," Saoirse said, turning her gaze back to me. I forced myself to look down at my plate.

"Her guards agreed with what Samantha and Ciarán told us," Niamh said.

"Where are they now? Finn and Seamus?" Samantha asked softly.

"They're still with Aodhan. The state of decay in Aoife's land is partially their doing, so they are going to help set things right," Saoirse said with an alluring smile.

Deaghlan leaned back and laughed. "Oh, you make it sound like they are such willing volunteers."

It was all I could do not to tell Deaghlan to keep his comments to himself. I picked up one of the cakes and stuffed it in my mouth.

It was light and fluffy, like a combination of the sticky sweetness of Baklava and the airy goodness of fried dough.

"I will need some time to reflect on what the future has in store," Saoirse said. When I looked up at her, her lips were glistening from whatever she was drinking. She raised her finger to her mouth and tapped her bottom lip. "Would you join me, Allison?"

My mouth dropped open, and I let out a surprised laugh. "Okay," I said slowly. Niamh's eyebrows quirked just enough that I knew she was startled, too.

I'll come with you.

I gave her a tiny nod.

"Do you want me to come?" Ethan asked, concerned.

I shook my head. "I'll be okay," I said. "Stay here and finish eating."

He didn't look convinced, but he nodded.

Niamh stood, and I trailed her and Saoirse to the door leading to the back side of the mountain. The sky was the light aqua of a tropical sea, which I'd learned meant it was still early in the day. The last time I'd been down here, Saoirse had shown me a vision of Ethan as Breanh's prisoner.

We followed Saoirse down the stone path through a garden burgeoning with flowers in all shades of reds, yellows and blues. Fruit trees gave the light breeze a pleasant fragrance.

At the edge of the garden, a stream flowed down the mountain, emptying into a clear pool. This was Danu's

Basin, the magical gift shared by the queens of each generation.

Saoirse sat on the stone bench set at the water's edge. Niamh and I sat on either side of her.

"Before you begin, I have to ask why Father is being so rude," Niamh said.

Saoirse, who looked like a paler, more delicate version of Niamh, smoothed her hand along her daughter's cheek.

"When he came home, your father was quite upset about how things went with Aodhan. Yes, I know all about what happened," she said, arching her brow.

"We were all upset. Father was being unreasonable."

"That may well be. But like I said, he was shaken up. He'd just finished relaying all the events from Liam's house, when Aodhan himself showed up with Seamus and Finn bound and gagged. It took all of my strength plus your own guards to keep him from ending Aodhan's life right then."

Niamh sucked in a sharp breath. "He wouldn't."

Saoirse cocked one dainty eyebrow, but didn't reply.

"Is that why Aodhan isn't here now? Because of what happened between him and Deaghlan?" I asked.

"Yes and no," Saoirse said. "I've asked Aodhan to keep an eye on things for me. Aoife's guards have been placed in fey globes for the time being."

A memory of something Deaghlan had said several days ago popped into my mind. Before I could ask Saoirse if he was right and she was the one who freed Aoife from her fey globe, Niamh shook her head.

Let her finish the story first.

"You aren't fond of Deaghlan," Saoirse said, looking at me, her eyes knowing. "He has a difficult personality most of the time." She laughed softly. "No one knows that more than me. But I have known him longer than you can probably fathom. We grew up together, the best of friends. I always hoped he would be my bond-mate, my partner. He didn't feel the same toward me. When I found out we were to be bonded, it was like a dream come true. For Deaghlan, it was like being bound forever to his little sister."

I sat in stunned silence. Saoirse, the beautiful, enigmatic leader of the Tuatha De Danaan, loved Deaghlan. And he didn't return her feelings.

"Ah, Allison. I see that look. Do not pity me. I am not human, therefore I am not a slave to my emotions. I only tell you this so you understand why I indulge Deaghlan."

Still unable to find the right thing to say, I simply nodded.

"Niamh, have I ever told you about my grandparents -- Manannán and Fand?"

"Not very much, Mother."

"Well, Manannán loved Fand. He gave her every luxury, anything she desired was hers if she just asked him for it.

"They ruled in Tír na n'Óg for thousands of years. In those days, war between the clans of this realm was a part of life. My grandfather spent much of his time away in battle."

"There are other clans?" I asked.

Saoirse's lips pressed together. "Not anymore. The Danaans are few, but the other clans haven't been heard from in more than two thousand years.

"My grandmother would go to the human realm while my grandfather was away. She fell in love with a man who, like Samantha, was from a Danaan and human coupling.

"When the Danaan armies my grandfather led defeated our greatest enemies, the Fomorians, he was weary. As you know, our kind do not die of old age. But when we have lived long enough to grow jaded with this world, our people move on to *Magh Mell*, across the Aimsirean Sea.

"My grandfather asked my grandmother to retire with him to *Magh Mell*, but she wouldn't go. He knew it was because of her feelings for another man. In a fit of jealousy, he wiped her memories of this man. Once their daughter, my mother, was settled as queen, they sailed across the sea, never to return.

"I believe the time has come for Deaghlan and I to make the journey to *Magh Mell*. He has refused, saying he's not ready. Unlike my grandmother, I don't think he hesitates for love. I've looked at the ways our future could play out, and there are only two ways I'll be able to convince him to join me. The first is if I use magic, like my grandfather." She paused, waiting for a reaction, but neither Niamh nor I said anything.

"The second is if Niamh is properly bonded and ready to be queen."

Niamh stood slowly, not taking her eyes off her mother. Her expression was a blank mask.

"Properly bonded to whom?" she asked.

Saoirse smoothed the material of her gown, unperturbed. "It is your duty as the first born princess, Niamh. You know that."

"That's not what I asked, Mother. I asked *to whom?*"

"I've accepted Aodhan's offer to restore our land, in part because I want him to prove his worthiness to your father."

"You're playing games with him?" Niamh's spine stiffened. "Father nearly killed him."

"He wouldn't have," Saoirse said, brushing her off.

"Even if Aodhan were to agree to it, he couldn't be king. He's not Danaan."

Saoirse tilted her head to the side, and when she spoke her voice was calm but firm. "Must I remind you who is queen?"

Niamh began pacing, her golden hair trailing behind her. A tiny thread of fear showed in her eyes.

"Aodhan has just spoken the first few words to me in decades, Mother. If you propose this to him now, he'll think it's my idea."

Saoirse stood and glided over to Niamh. "My darling," she said softly. "My plans are not so impulsive as that."

"What do you have in mind?" Niamh asked.

"Come sit. Let me show you what I've seen."

Niamh followed Saoirse back to the bench and sat. Saoirse raised her arms toward the pool, causing the water to churn. As she closed her eyes, mist rose from the surface. With a sudden motion, her hands dropped back down. The mist disappeared and the water was smooth like glass. A vision came to the surface.

It was of a gently sloping hillside at night with people milling around everywhere. An enormous bonfire was on top of the hill with smaller fires and torches lit all over the landscape. I walked up the hill with Ethan and Liam. We were searching for something, but I couldn't make out what we were whispering to each other over the sounds of drumming and the crackling fires.

I'd dreamt of this, but my memory of the dream was hazy.

Saoirse murmured something and held out her hands again. "This isn't what I wanted to show you. I haven't seen this vision before," she whispered.

On the water's surface, we approached a large stone sculpture. It was shaped like a giant popsicle and came up to my chest when I stood in front of it. Liam grabbed my arm before I could touch the stone. Familiar laughter rose above the sounds in the distance. *Aoife.*

Before we could see what happened next, Deaghlan's voice rang out from the path. "Saoirse!"

The water bubbled and the vision disappeared.

"I'm going back to make sure Aodhan has things under control," Deaghlan said, his voice laced with venom.

Saoirse glanced at me, her lip quirking just slightly. "Very well," she said to Deaghlan.

Niamh jumped up. "I'll go with you."

"What, are you going to babysit me now, too? Not necessary," Deaghlan said, turning on his heel.

Niamh hurried after him.

Saoirse sighed next to me. "Do you know what that was in the vision, Allison?" she said.

"I have no idea. But I have seen it before, in a dream."

"Interesting," she said, her eyes narrowing. "That was the Hill of Tara, in Ireland. Does that mean anything to you?"

I shook my head. "Not really. I mean, I've heard of it, but I don't know very much about it."

Saoirse smiled. "The standing stone we saw was a gift from my great grandfather to the High King of Ireland a great many years ago. It's known as the Stone of Destiny."

"What's it for?"

"Human legends say it cries out when it senses the true king of Ireland. But it's far more valuable than that. It's the last piece of raw háillan in existence."

Fháillan. The metal worn by Aodhan, Liam and Niamh to protect them from iron.

"Did Niamh tell you Samantha overheard Aoife talking about fháillan mines?"

Saoirse's unusual eyes widened. "She didn't."

"All she said was that Aoife was talking to her guards, about binding rituals and mines. Samantha didn't know anything else, she didn't even know what fháillan mines were."

Saoirse's eyes darkened and became unfocused. I didn't know what to do. "Saoirse?"

She remained perfectly still a moment longer before her eyes regained their light.

"I apologize," she said, taking a breath. "I just wanted to see if I could make sense of what you told me in addition to what we saw in the water."

"And could you?" I asked.

Saoirse looked at me as if she wasn't sure how much she should say. "Niamh told me about Aoife performing a binding ritual. I'm afraid that's true. Aoife knows the only way to perform such strong magic is with a large amount of fháillan. There are no fháillan mines in Tír na n'Óg, so she will perform it at the next best place, the Hill of Tara, at the

Stone of Destiny."

Even though I'd known this was a possibility from what Samantha had told us, hearing Saoirse say it with so much certainty caused my heart to stutter.

"When? Can you tell when she's going to do it?"

She glanced down at the tips of her slippers. When she looked back up, her expression was neutral. "There are four great fire festivals on Tara. One for each of the seasons. The next one will take place on Samhain, also known as Halloween."

"Halloween? That's over a month away, so we're not too late?"

Saoirse stood, and the unreadable expression on her face twisted my insides. Did she know something she wasn't telling me? I followed her back up the hill to the Bruidhean, tears of frustration burning behind my eyes.

We found Liam and Ethan still sitting in the same place we'd left them. Samantha paced at the end of the dining room like a caged animal. Her hair stuck out in every direction from her constant abuse.

Liam's hopeful expression caused something to unravel inside me. Anger, frustration and fear flooded through me. I pictured my mother's face as she looked at Liam with pure love in her eyes. I wasn't sure what, but I knew I simply had to figure out a way to set things right. And the only way to do that was to deal with Aoife myself.

Chapter Twelve

Liam stayed quiet while Saoirse told him what we'd learned. Something churned in his eyes. Anger laced with regret that mirrored my own. Tension coiled in his forearms as he closed and opened his fists on the table.

"It's simple, then," he said. "I'll go to Tara and stop her."

"Of course, Liam," Saoirse said, her smile vague.

"Wait," I said. "It's not enough to just stop her. We have to get the amulet and destroy it."

Liam stared at me a moment, then nodded. "Whatever it takes."

"How much time has passed in our world?" I asked.

"Just under a week," Liam said.

"It's still September. Halloween isn't for six more weeks," I said, thinking. "What if we could find Aoife in the meantime?"

"You can try," Saoirse said. "Although, if she doesn't want to be found, you may not be very successful."

"What about Dublin? If she has a portal that leads there, wouldn't that be the first place we should look?"

"If it were me, and I was hiding, I know I wouldn't go to the most obvious place," Ethan said, shrugging.

"That's a good point," Liam said.

"What else do we have to go on?" I asked.

"Maybe she's still in Thunder Bay," Samantha said.

"Hmm, I didn't even think of that," I said. "There's no one there to get in her way, either. Her guards and Niamh's are all here."

"I think you'd be wasting your time," Saoirse said. "Stay here for another day or two and make plans. Then leave for Dublin and it will be the end of October."

I looked at Saoirse, puzzled. "One day would be equal to a month?" I asked.

"Yes, one more day. The sun must rise and set three times in this world to equal one moon cycle in yours."

I squeezed my eyes shut. A month there would be three days here. As much as I hated to admit it, it would make sense to wait the extra day. I didn't think I could make it six more weeks out there, knowing what the future held. After all, Saoirse said that the visions in Danu's Basin were absolute. So even if we went running all over the globe, we'd still end up in Tara on Halloween.

"Okay. We'll come up with a plan here. I wasn't taking the time difference into account."

Liam's jaw hardened, but he nodded. "Very well."

"She's planning on channeling power from the Stone of Destiny, right?" I asked Saoirse.

Saoirse inclined her head.

"I couldn't see her in the vision, but I could hear her. I'm guessing that means she was glamoured."

"We'll be able to see through that. It won't be a problem," Liam said quietly.

"Do you think she'll be expecting us?" I asked.

"Even I don't know the answer to that," Saoirse said.

"Is it possible for us to sneak up on her?" Samantha said.

"No," Liam said. "She'll be able to sense me and probably you girls, too."

"But not me?" Ethan asked.

Liam shook his head, his brows furrowing. "No, she won't be able to sense anything from you."

"So, it might be possible for Ethan to sneak up behind

her and subdue her?"

Saoirse got that far off look in her eyes again. Everyone at the table stared at her while she was lost in her vision. When her eyes refocused, she shook her head. "I'm having a hard time seeing Aoife's future. It could be the iron in her system, I just don't know."

"Iron blocks your visions?" Samantha said, cocking her head to the side.

Saoirse looked at Samantha. "It's possible."

I never knew iron was so dangerous, Samantha projected into my mind.

I gave her a sympathetic smile. *How could you have known?*

I thought of Liam, weakened by the steel dagger while we were in Thunder Bay. Aodhan had brought Aengus, the one who stabbed Liam, to his knees with steel chains.

"That's it," I said and everyone looked at me. "If Liam and Samantha distract Aoife, Ethan and I can trap her with steel chains."

Saoirse pressed her lips together and Liam looked like he was considering my idea.

"Yeah," Ethan said. "I'll do whatever you need."

"Once she's immobilized, we take the amulet and destroy it," I said.

Liam nodded. "It could work," he said.

"I recognize she's done wrong. But I must ask you not to harm Aoife," Saoirse said.

"Niamh asked the same, and I understand," I said, glancing at Liam. He looked like he wanted to disagree. I could understand that, too.

For the next few hours, we worked out the logistics of our plan. Aoife's portal would bring us to a castle in the outskirts of Dublin. If we left tomorrow evening, we would be in Ireland with plenty of time for Halloween. After we picked up the supplies we needed, we would head north to the Hill of Tara.

Throughout the day, serving men and women brought food and drinks to the table. I marveled at how much the Danaan's lives revolved around eating and drinking. I also knew there was another piece, but I had a feeling it had been tamped down while the humans were visiting. Danaans were an amorous people. Where humans liked to show their affection for those they cared about, at least some of the time, Danaans were all about pleasure. Giving pleasure, receiving pleasure either by food or drink or sex, it didn't matter.

Once we'd gone over the plans with painstaking detail, Saoirse rose from her chair. "If you'll excuse me, I'm going to take a bath before our evening meal."

"That sounds like a good idea. I'll do the same," Liam said as he stood, too.

Before Saoirse left the table, she raised a hand and several of the men and women who served us throughout our meeting appeared.

"Our guests would like to bathe before dinner. Would you show them to the bathing pools?" Saoirse said as she turned to leave.

We followed the servants up to the guest quarters. Fresh clothes and blanket-soft towels were laid out on the bed in the room Ethan and I had slept in.

Ethan picked up the button-down shirt and drawstring pants and smirked. It definitely wasn't something he'd usually wear, but I couldn't imagine anything looking bad on him.

"So, do we all go to a community bath or something?" he asked.

I laughed. "Not exactly. Streams run through the mountain. The bathing pools are pretty secluded."

He grinned. "Good thing, I wouldn't want to indulge your fantasies."

I threw one of the towels at him, but I smiled at his teasing tone. "Whatever. My fantasies are much more creative than you in the tub."

His eyebrow quirked up. "Is that so?" he asked, a devilish gleam in his eye.

Trying to keep from laughing, I nodded.

He came over to where I stood in front of the door. "Liar," he said, effectively boxing me in.

I shrugged, because honestly, I could hardly breathe with him standing so close, especially with that look on his face.

"I'd like to hear more about these fantasies," he said, stepping forward so my back was pressed against the door.

"Oh, please —" I started to say, but Ethan pressed one finger to my lips. Outside the door, Samantha called out my name.

"We'll talk about your fantasies later," he said. "I think you better go take a bath first, though."

I shook my head. "Sure we will." I ducked under his arm, grabbed my clothes and towel and hurried out the door.

Samantha and I walked into the stone chamber lined with hand-carved basins. Down the stone stairs on the far wall, a small river ran with private alcoves built in for bathing. Liam and Ethan had given us the bathing pools first, for some human privacy. The Danaan in residence weren't anywhere around, likely for the same reason.

As we washed, I heard Samantha's heavy sigh in the space next to me. "I thought Ciarán would have come by now," she said.

I didn't say anything right away. "Maybe he doesn't want to start a fight."

Samantha snorted. "That would be a first."

"I'm definitely not an expert when it comes to guys. Not even close."

"Yeah, right," she said. "Ethan follows you around like

he's a puppy and you're a T-bone."

I took a breath, unable to smother the laugh that bubbled up. "You are so wrong," I said.

"Anyone with eyes can see the way he watches you. I wish Ciarán looked at me like that. Most of the time, I don't think he even *likes* me."

Ignoring the flutter in my chest, I asked, "Why would he be with you if he didn't like you?"

She didn't say anything for so long, I didn't think she would answer. "I don't know,"she said finally.

We didn't speak after that. When we went back to the guest quarters, Samantha mumbled a goodbye. I went into my room feeling a little bit down, wishing I'd known what to say to make her feel better.

I sat on the bed and smoothed my hands down the gown I'd been given. I rarely wore dresses, but I didn't mind this one. The smooth, amethyst material was as comfortable as a nightgown, but fit me perfectly.

"Look at you," Ethan said from the doorway.

A flush crept over my cheeks. I looked up and he was leaning against the doorframe wearing the linen shirt and khaki drawstring pants. He looked like a model on a romance novel.

"Right back at you," I said as I stood.

"I like the purple," he said, circling around me.

"Thanks."

"So," he said. "They're going to stuff us with some more food, we sleep, then we're going to check in with Niamh and Aodhan. Are you nervous?"

"A little." I shrugged. "Okay, more than a little. I just want to do something. It's the waiting that kills me."

He smoothed my hair back from my face. "Our plan is awesome, you know. Aoife will never expect me to be there. She'll never know what hit her."

"Yeah," I said, nodding. I hoped I sounded more confident than I felt. I couldn't imagine how it would be waiting six weeks to finally make a move.

There was a light knock and Liam stuck his head in the doorway. "Ready to head down?" he asked. I could see Samantha just over his shoulder.

Ethan glanced at me and gestured for me to go first with his chin. "Yep, this is the longest I've gone without eating since we got here," he said.

"Just a warning, when we go home, food is going to taste like sawdust compared to the food here," I said.

Liam led all of us to the large gathering hall. The walls were covered in blue fabric, embroidered with flowering trees and twisting vines. Fey lights were suspended high above, giving the room a comfortable glow.

Men and women stood around in groups, talking and laughing. In their hands were chalices filled with sparkling gold wine.

An unusually long table filled one side of the room. Ten high back chairs were lined up on either side, and Saoirse sat at the head of the table.

When she saw us, her smile was breathtaking. I realized how long I'd spent in Saoirse's presence today without becoming baffled just from looking at her. Had I grown immune to her charm? Or maybe she had toned it down for a while. Either way, I was glad. The memory of being enraptured was not one I liked to think about.

We ate roasted meat and vegetables followed by fruit and scones with cream. Every bite was so delicious I was tempted to lick my fingers clean. Conversation took place all around us, but mostly Samantha, Liam, Ethan and I just listened as men told stories and women laughed. As we ate our dessert, a trio in the corner began playing music. One played a flute like Aodhan carried with him, one a drum and one played fiddle.

Couples left the table to dance. They moved with a fluid grace that no human could ever accomplish.

"Would you care to dance?" Saoirse asked us.

My eyes widened and I shook my head. I could dance a little, but no way was I going out there. Even a highly trained ballerina would look clumsy among the Danaan.

Saoirse rose and bid us goodnight before gracefully joining the dancers.

We went back up to the guest quarters in silence. Anxious energy had been building inside me all day and I wished I could go for a run to work some of it off.

I fell back onto one of the couches and covered my face with my arms. I felt Ethan sit beside me and nudge me with his elbow. I opened one eye and he gave me a curious look.

"Are you getting tired?" he asked.

I groaned. "No, not at all. That's the problem," I said. "I'm a nervous wreck."

Liam and Samantha took seats on the other couches. Liam leaned back and ran his hands through his hair.

Samantha jumped up suddenly. "He's here," she said, her voice just above a whisper. She turned her head and looked at me, eyes wide. "Ciarán's here."

I started to say something, but she took off down the hallway. Liam chuckled and sat up.

"I was just thinking about how Aodhan and Deaghlan are faring," he said.

"Oh man," I said. "It must be a fiasco."

"I don't get Deaghlan. I know he's supposed to be wicked powerful and everything, but he's such a tool," Ethan said.

Liam snickered. "I guess living for a millennium turned him that way. According to Aodhan, he was still admirable when he first met him, about four hundred years ago."

"Hard to believe," I said. "Can we head over to see what's going on first thing tomorrow?"

"Absolutely," Liam said. "Sitting here isn't doing us any good."

He stood and stretched. "I'll be off to bed, then."

Ethan sighed, rubbing a hand along his jaw. Once Liam

was gone, he slid a look at me. "I wouldn't mind hearing about those fantasies of yours now," he said, waggling his eyebrows.

Laughing, I gave him a light shove. "I told you that's not going to happen."

He pushed off the couch, grabbing my hand. Before I could protest, he pulled me to my feet.

"We'll see," he said, ushering me toward our room. *Our room?*

Kicking the door shut, he clasped my cheeks. His hands were warm and smooth but they still sent a shiver through me. He stared down at me intently, and my breath caught.

He lowered his head, kissing me softly. I gasped at the sensations that rippled through me and his hands slid down to my hips, pulling me toward him. Without realizing it, we ended up at the foot of the bed. I pulled back a little and dragged in a breath.

"What's wrong?" he asked, resting his forehead against mine.

I cleared my throat. "Nothing," I said and tried to smile.

He moved his hands to my lower back and turned us so that when he sat down I was on his lap. "I think I know what this is about."

"I'm serious, nothing's wrong," I said.

He gave me a skeptical look. "I can't keep my hands off you, and I won't apologize for that. But I have zero expectations, okay?"

I nodded, internally kicking myself for being so inexperienced.

Ethan brought his lips back to mine, and this time I didn't hesitate. I brought my hands up to his shoulders and positioned myself so my knees were on either side of his hips. Our bodies melded together perfectly. I sucked in a breath when he slid his fingers under the hem of the gown and skimmed the backs of my knees.

"Can we take this off?" he asked, between kisses.

I froze and Ethan pulled back this time. "You can keep your underwear on. I just want to feel you."

The way he said it caused my heart to jolt. I leaned back and let him pull the silky material up and over my head. He tossed it to the side, eyes never leaving mine. His hands slid up the backs of my thighs and I pulled his mouth back to mine. His hands came up to unbutton his shirt and I pushed them away so I could do them myself.

I felt his lips curve into a smile against mine, and in one motion, he flipped us so I was on my back and he hovered over me. I placed my hands on his chest to pull the shirt down over his shoulders. His skin felt as smooth and perfect as I'd always imagined it would. I whimpered, making me want to turn away, but I could tell Ethan liked it by the way his hands tightened on my hips.

His lips slid down my cheek to my neck and he trailed feather-light kisses down to my shoulder. "You are so incredibly beautiful," he whispered into my neck.

I shivered and tried to regain normal, steady breaths.

"Do you know how many times I've imagined the way your body would feel against mine?" he said, easing off of me and lying on his side.

I tried to speak, but couldn't.

He shook his head and draped his arm over my bare stomach. "You don't have to say anything. I just wanted you to know."

I licked my lips. "It's…been the same for me," I said softly.

He smiled down at me and kissed my temple. "You're worth the wait."

We talked some more, not about anything important or life-threatening. Just little things. Then he tucked me under the covers in just my bra and undies, kissing me again until I was dizzy.

When he pulled back, he smiled down at me and kissed my nose. "Get some rest," he said.

I sighed and rolled onto my side. He chuckled and wrapped his arm around me, pulling me back against him. Before long I was lulled to sleep by the sound of his steady breathing.

Chapter Thirteen

While we were eating breakfast the next morning, we heard raised voices in the hallway. Saoirse stood and gestured to the guards standing by the door. They opened the double doors and two of Niamh's guards, Niall and Bláithín, whom I'd met in Thunder Bay, pointed their weapons at Samantha and Ciarán.

Saoirse gave her most serene smile to the company, an enormously powerful gesture. Without a word, both of Niamh's guards lowered their weapons and bowed their heads. Ciarán did the same.

I met Samantha's eyes. *What happened?* I asked in my thoughts.

Her eyes widened. *We were just coming in to have breakfast and these two freaked when they saw us. That's all I know.*

"Welcome, Niall and Bláithín. Is everything okay out here?" Saoirse said in her honey-smooth voice.

Niall sucked in a breath. "Ciarán was in Thunder Bay. He was one of the blood-drainers," he said.

Ciarán slid a contemptuous glance at Niall. "That's where you're wrong, old friend. I didn't harm a single human in Thunder Bay. I want no part of that."

Saoirse's calm expression didn't falter as she walked toward them. "It's the truth, Niall. I can confirm it."

Niall tucked his shoulder-length chestnut hair behind

one ear and continued to stare at Ciarán. "I apologize, my lady," he said.

"No apology necessary," she said. "You were just trying to protect us. Come, join us at the table."

When they were all seated, Bláithín spoke. "We have come to ask for a favor on behalf of Aodhan and Niamh."

Saoirse nodded, gesturing for her to continue.

Bláithín licked her lips and glanced quickly at Ciarán and Samantha. "Aodhan has put Aoife's entire household to work. He has the healers restoring the trees and any of the wild creatures who were affected by the iron pollution. The others are removing the dead trees and planting new ones. He would like to ask if you could send any other healers to assist them."

Saoirse beamed at this. "Of course. I will send my most gifted healers immediately." She frowned for a second and looked at Liam. "Eithne is in the human realm?"

"Yes. She and Diarmuid are guarding the portal," he said.

"No matter. I have others who are nearly as gifted."

"Would you like us to go back and pass the news to Eithne?" Ciarán asked. Samantha whipped around to look at him.

"I thought you were coming with me?" she asked. "We'll never make it back in time if we go through the portal."

Liam cleared his throat. "Samantha, bringing Eithne back here is important. I'm sure you can go with Ciarán and still make it to the Stone of Destiny in time for Samhain, excuse me, Halloween."

Samantha didn't seem convinced. She pushed her hands into her hair and shook her head. "Whatever you need," she muttered.

"Sam… " Ciarán began, but when Samantha looked at him, her lips were so tightly compressed with exasperation that he didn't finish.

The air in the room was thick with tension, and at exactly the same time, Liam and I pushed up from the table. I chuckled, easing the strained silence.

"If there's nothing else, we should be going," Liam said.

"What are your plans, Liam?" Bláithín asked, pushing her short, black hair back from her forehead.

Swallowing, Liam said, "We're headed to see how things are with Aodhan, actually."

"Oh, you're in for a treat," Niall said, leaning back in his chair. He laughed and twisted his lips into a wry smile.

Bláithín put a hand up to her mouth, trying to stifle her snicker.

Liam approached Saoirse at the head of the table. "Thank you for your insight, as always," he said.

"As far as I can see, there is no reason your plan won't work," she said. "Please remember what I've asked of you."

Liam inclined his head, but didn't say anything. I gave Saoirse a smile and an awkward wave before saying goodbye to everyone at the table.

"We'll be along soon," Niall said, clapping Liam on the shoulder.

Liam nodded and we followed him out of the dining room. As we left, I turned to give Samantha a final wave, but she wouldn't meet my gaze. *I'll see you in Ireland*, I said in my mind and walked toward the door.

Liam was a wonderful storyteller. As we crossed through glens and over hills, he told us tales he heard as a child. Girls turned to geese and men with magical fish. We were soon captivated.

We didn't speak of Aoife or the geis. Nobody said a word about the task ahead. I was glad, too. Knowing we must go up against Aoife was one thing, but dwelling on it was something else entirely.

Before long we came to the twisting bramble wall that had ensnared me and Aodhan the last time we followed this path. There were men and women cutting it down with axes and long knives that looked like some sort of swords.

In the center, a path wide enough for six people was cut through. The sickening smell of the dried up vines made me light-headed, but I kept my sleeve over my nose and was able to keep walking. I warned Ethan and Liam that the last time I'd walked through here, the odor seeping out of the vines made me dizzy and barely able to walk. Liam greeted the workers as we passed, but most just smiled sadly and looked away.

"The taint has reached more than the land," Liam said once we'd made it to the other side of the thorny forest. "Aoife's people have lost their spirit."

I looked over my shoulder at them hacking and sawing. Their faces were lifeless and dull.

Beyond the briars, the land was as colorless as the people. Dry, brittle grass crunched under our feet as we walked. There were no flowers or leaves to speak of, only dead and fallen trees across the flat, parched land. More groups were cutting down the trees and removing the trunks.

As we got closer to the cliff that held the entrance to Aoife's household, the ground grew sandier. The face of the cliff sat high above a rolling sea. To get to the entrance of the cave, we followed a steep, narrow path.

Liam went ahead without hesitation and I remembered this had once been his home. I hugged the cliff as we walked, not wanting to see the rocky shore below.

Inside the cave, fey lights dotted the path leading to the front doors. I could hear voices and movement below even though I couldn't see anyone yet.

The round double doors were open and a group of women carrying trays of tiny plants walked through. They hurried past, keeping their heads down.

"Those were some of our healers," Liam said, watching them hasten up the path.

"They're replacing the trees that have been lost," I said. "Do you remember what it was like here before it became polluted?"

"Oh, yes," Liam said, running his fingers through his hair. "The whole seaside was covered with billowing grass and wildflowers. Clusters of trees dotted the landscape, it was breath taking."

I wished I could have seen it as he described, rather than the wasteland I'd seen.

"How long has it been like this?" Ethan asked.

"Not very long," Liam said as he opened another door that lead into a large gathering room. He glanced back at us. "A year or two in this world."

The room was a flurry of activity. Deaghlan sat at one end in a large chair set up on a dais. A line of people stood waiting for their turn to speak with him. He looked like a true king, oddly enough, listening to what the people had to say. His face lacked the utter boredom and disdain it usually held. He looked genuinely concerned with what was going on.

Aodhan stood at the head of a large, round table. Four men stood around the table, watching as he pointed at a map. And by his side was Niamh.

I caught Liam's eye and he looked just as surprised as me to see Aodhan and Niamh working together. Niamh's head jerked up and she gave us a smile so small, it was just a slight twitch of her lips.

A girl approached the table carrying a tray of silver handled mugs. Niamh smiled at her and took two, handing one to Aodhan.

"What kind of alternate reality have we entered?" I asked Liam with wide eyes.

He didn't say anything, just smirked as we walked toward the table. Aodhan looked up and gave us one of his rare grins.

"Good to see you, old friend," he said, clapping Liam on the back.

"Things are going well here, I take it?" Liam asked, returning the gesture.

Niamh nodded and took a sip from her mug. "Quite well. Aodhan is keeping Father busy. I haven't seen him this way since —" she faltered. "Not in a long time."

"I can't take the credit for that," Aodhan said. "The people aren't so afraid now they know something is being done to help them. Deaghlan has really stepped up. I wouldn't believe it if I weren't seeing it with my own eyes."

"Me either," I said, glancing back to where Deaghlan sat nodding at something a woman was saying to him.

"What did my mother have to say after I left?" Niamh asked.

"Well, you saw the vision of the Stone of Destiny?" I asked.

She nodded and ushered us into the corner of the room where we could have privacy. Aodhan angled his body toward me, paying attention.

"Just like Samantha told us, Aoife is planning a binding ceremony. It'll be done on Halloween at the Stone of Destiny."

"She'll draw power from the stone," Aodhan said quietly, nodding.

"Right," I said. "Our plan is to go there tonight. We'll get there just in time for the Fire Festival of Samhain."

Aodhan rubbed his jaw. "How do you plan on stopping her?"

"Well," I said drawing in my bottom lip. "Liam is going to approach her while Ethan and I sneak up from behind. Ethan's going to use steel chains to hold her while I grab her necklace."

Niamh nodded. "That sounds like a good plan. Just be sure to stay out of her sight before she begins."

"That's what I was thinking," Aodhan said, nodding.

"The whole plan could fall through if she sees you too soon."

"Agreed," I said.

"We saw lots getting done on our way here," Liam said.

Niamh slid a hesitant glance at Aodhan. "Yes. It's a work in progress, but at least things are moving forward."

"What's going to happen when the land is restored? Will Saoirse seal the portals?" I asked.

"Well," Niamh said. "That's difficult to say. From what she's told us, I'm sure she'll seal at least one or two of them."

"I'd like to know how you brought on such a change in Deaghlan," I said to Aodhan.

He shrugged, his hands going up to smooth his cropped hair. "It's like I said, once he pulled his head out last night, people felt like they could come to him with things they'd been too afraid to speak to Aoife about. It's been an interesting day, to say the least."

"Mother knew what she was doing, sending Aodhan here," Niamh said.

Aodhan chuckled. "If she'd asked Deaghlan to take care of this problem directly, the outcome would have been different. Saoirse is very subtle."

I thought about that for a second. Aodhan was right. If Saoirse had asked Deaghlan, he would have avoided it. By asking Aodhan, it was like lighting a fire directly under Deaghlan. How that must have burned him.

"Ciarán and Samantha will be coming here at some point this evening," Liam said. "Samantha wants to be there when we go to Tara."

Niamh's brow furrowed. She looked at Liam and I could tell they were having a telepathic conversation.

"Allison," Aodhan said, his expression solemn. "Be careful. I wish I could be there with you, but I'm sure Ethan will look after you."

Ethan shifted from one foot to the other, but he nodded.

"I'll be careful," I said, laughing. I nudged Ethan in the side to be sure he realized Aodhan wasn't trying to offend him. He gave me a lopsided grin and I knew he was fine.

Aoife's portal was in her bedchamber. Niamh led us upstairs and past a series of closed doors until we reached the end of the hallway. She glanced at Liam quickly before opening the door. I wished I didn't have to go in, it felt wrong to be in Aoife's bedroom.

I took a breath and slowly walked in. The room was eerily quiet and I suppressed a shudder. A single fey light cast the room in a pale glow. Niamh flicked her wrist and dozens of the tiny lights came on around the room. It felt like a hotel room once it was lit up, everything in perfect order.

Niamh crossed the room to a crimson velvet curtain draped across the wall. She flicked her wrist and the curtains parted to reveal a magnificent mural painted on the stone. Whimsical swirls and flourishes came together to be a sort of map. Mountains, lakes and other landmarks were drawn in detail across the surface. In the center of the map was the artist's rendition of the Bruidhean. And just above that was a handprint decorated with ancient markings like runes.

"Are you ready?" she asked.

Ethan and I nodded. "We are," Liam said.

Niamh regarded the three of us and smiled. "To your safe return," she whispered.

Liam held his palm flush against the handprint and a pure, concentrated white light enveloped the bedchamber. I threw my arm up to cover my eyes and stepped forward until the light dimmed.

When I reopened my eyes I saw crumbling stone walls surrounding us. A stone paved floor was covered in rubble and debris. This was Aoife's home in Ireland?

Liam must have seen my surprise. "Welcome to Castle

Tamhnach."

"This is it?" I asked.

Liam blinked. "It's glamoured. Look closer."

Ethan came to my side, his forehead scrunched up with confusion. I tried to see past the glamour. Once I concentrated, the ruins melted away, leaving behind a room with a vaulted post and beam ceiling. The stone flooring was clear of the debris I thought I'd seen. In the center of the room was a dark pine table and benches with a lush oriental rug underneath. One small window near the ceiling allowed daylight to shine on an enormous stone fireplace, circa the Middle Ages, where a cooking pot and kettle were hung.

"This place is amazing," I said, awestruck.

"It is?" Ethan said, arching a brow.

"I wish you could see it, it's unbelievable," I said as I walked to the table where a stoneware vase was filled with poufy white flowers.

"It's kept glamoured to look like a ruin and marked as condemned by the Irish authorities," Liam said.

Ethan nodded, but remained rooted to his spot.

A short, heavy woman bustled into the room. "Oh, Liam. Good to see you, love," she said in a thick Irish brogue as she hurried over to him and grasped his cheeks with her plump hands.

"Ah, hello Maire," Liam said warmly.

"And, who've we here?" the woman asked, turning toward Ethan and me.

"This is Allison," Liam said looking at me. "My daughter. And this is her friend Ethan."

"Daughter, you say? Well, the blessings of God be on you, aren't you a beauty," Maire said with a
smile.

"This is Maire O'Reilly, caretaker of Tamhnach."

"Nice to meet you," I said, smiling.

"And, Ethan. What a lovely young man you are," Maire said, fluttering her lashes at him.

I smirked at Ethan as he held out his hand to her. She made a delighted sound when he raised her hand to his lips. Always the charmer.

"We've come with an important errand this time," Liam said.

Maire sighed. "Yes, the Lady told me to be expecting you," she said.

"Oh?" Liam said, his brows shooting up.

"Yes, she isn't here at the moment. But she said you'd be along shortly," Maire said. "Now, why don't you come home with me? Are you thirsty? You must be hungry."

Liam glanced back at me, his jaw clenching. "We're actually in quite a bit of a hurry, I'm sorry to say. So I thank you, but we'll just be on our way."

"What a pity. I'll be getting on home to feed Mr. O'Reilly his lunch, anyway."

She bustled toward the door and we followed her into a galley kitchen with the same stone walls and floors. There were no modern appliances or food to speak of, but it was as immaculate as a museum.

Maire pulled a set of keys out of her pocket and opened the door in the back of the kitchen, waiting as we walked out. The sun was hiding behind clouds, and a fine mist was falling. After she turned the key in the lock, Maire reached over and grabbed Liam's hands. "It's been good to see you, my boy. I do hope you'll come by and visit me before you leave."

"Ah, we'll see what we can do. But, Maire?"

"Yes, love?" Maire asked while she pulled her silk scarf up over her hair.

Liam looked at the damp ground and ran his hands over his hair. "If you see her again, don't mention you saw us, all right?"

Maire frowned, dropping Liam's hands. "If that's what you'd like, I won't say a word about it."

"It was so nice to meet you, Maire," I told her, trying to

keep things from getting too awkward.

"And you as well, dear." She gave Liam one last look and hurried down the long path leading to a road at the bottom of the hill.

When she was out of hearing range, Liam cursed. "She told Maire to be expecting us, that doesn't bode well."

I sighed. "There's nothing we can do about that. We have to just stick to our plan."

"Let's find a newspaper, we need to know for sure what the date is," Liam said waving his hand toward the road below.

We didn't talk as we walked down the little path. I took a minute to take in the breathtaking view. I could see mountains up beyond the castle and rolling hills below. Just like I'd always heard, everything was green and rocky.

The meandering tree-lined road led us past an old red school house and a thatch-roofed cottage, up over an old hump-backed railway bridge to a quaint village. The streets were lined with welcoming store fronts and quaint restaurants and pubs. Liam led us to a door with a 'Kemp's Pub' sign hanging overhead.

Inside, the place was a perfect combination of antique and modern decor. By the polished mahogany bar sat a newspaper rack. Liam picked one up and his eyes scanned for the date.

"October 31," he said, nodding.

"Geez, talk about cutting it close," I said, looking around the pub for a clock. It was 12:35 p.m.

"At least we still have plenty of time to get up to Tara," Ethan said.

The hostess approached us with a welcoming smile. "Good afternoon, and welcome to Kemp's," she said in a lilting Irish brogue. "Would you like to be seated or will you be eating at the bar?"

Liam looked at me and shrugged. "Ah, thank you. We'll take a table."

After we'd been seated, Liam stretched his legs out in front of him. "Twenty minutes until one," he said quietly, like he was talking to himself. "We'll want to be at Tara by half past four at the latest. The sun usually sets around five in October."

"Fair enough," I said, picking up a menu. There was a lot of seafood and I knew chips meant french fries here. The prices were all in euros. "How are we going to pay for anything?" I whispered.

Liam rubbed the back of his neck. "Leave that to me," he said without meeting my eyes.

The waitress came and brought us a pitcher of water. "I'm Emma and I'll be your server today. Can I start you off with an appetizer?"

"No, thank you," I said. "We're just going to order our meals."

"I don't know if I can trust the Irish with lasagna," Ethan said, trying to get a rise out of us.

"Oh, no," Liam said, beefing up his brogue. "Ye better order the only thing we Irish know how to prepare, a heapin' plate o' corned beef an' cabbage."

I had just taken a sip of the water in front of me and had to cover my mouth to keep from spitting it out. Ethan and Liam both broke out into boisterous laughter at the cliché.

"You can't go wrong with fish and chips," I said, still laughing and handed my menu to Emma.

"Right you are," Liam said, closing his as well. "I'll have the same."

"Well, I'm going to be different and get the Striped Bass," Ethan said, passing his menu to the waitress. "When we went fishing a few years ago off the Cape, the striper we caught made good eating."

"All right, sounds good," I said.

The waitress smiled, and flirted a little with Ethan and Liam. She probably thought we were a bunch of college grads on vacation. They made each other laugh as though they were. I smiled watching them tease each other after she left. It helped break up the tension over the activities waiting for us.

"Is there a hardware store close by where we can pick up the chains?" Ethan asked Liam once she walked away.

Liam stiffened, no doubt from the mention of our business here. "Taney Hardware is just a block away."

"Do you have any idea how long it takes to get to Tara from here?" I asked.

"It's just about a forty-minute car ride. You two can take a cab. If it's all the same, I'd prefer going on foot."

I frowned. "Do you really think it's a good idea for us to split up?"

"Oh, no worries there. I'll find you quickly."

I wasn't so sure, but I knew being in a car for any length of time made Liam nauseous, even with the fháillan band around his arm warding off all that steel.

"Okay, then that's what we'll do," I said, just as the waitress arrived with our food.

We ate in silence. I couldn't stop looking at the clock above the bar. The minute hand was racing forward, I could feel every tick of the second hand with the beat of my heart.

I turned and glanced at Liam. He pushed his plate away without having eaten very much. His jaw was carved from stone and his fists were balled up on top of the table.

I felt anxiety blossom in my belly. We still had more than two hours until we had to leave for Tara. I was half-wanting to just get it over with and half-wishing the time would never come. While we were making plans, I'd been focusing on being positive, not stopping to consider what would happen if it didn't work. Now the fear of failing gnawed away at me.

Saoirse wouldn't have let us come here if she didn't think we'd be able to succeed. That's what I kept telling myself. I wished I understood how her visions worked better. She could see the future with absolute certainty, couldn't she? So why were there no guarantees we'd achieve what we came here to do?

I shook my head to clear out the negative thoughts. That way led to madness.

Eventually the waitress came back with our check. I looked at the clock for what must have been the millionth time. An hour had passed. It was now 1:35. Time was officially standing still.

Liam picked up a napkin and tore it into four pieces. He crumpled the pieces in his hand and put his hands in his lap. When the waitress walked past, he flagged her over. Picking up the check she'd left, he passed it back to her along with the crumpled napkin. "Keep the change," he said with a charming smile.

Stunned, I just sat there watching her take the torn up napkin as if it were the biggest tip she'd ever received.

"No way, man," Ethan said. "That is so wrong. But so cool."

"I don't do it often, I assure you. But there are times when it comes in handy. Don't let it bother you, Allison. I'll send a large check to make up for it when we get back home."

I raised my hands. "Hey, whatever works." Liam's moral fiber was the least of my worries. I just needed to keep him from becoming Aoife's drone.

"You might want to take a few of these so we can get the chains," Ethan said, stuffing a handful of napkins into Liam's palm with a smirk.

I shook my head as I got up and headed for the exit.

We walked down the cobbled sidewalk to the hardware store. Liam's steps faltered when we walked through the door. Of course the place was packed with steel. In the first aisle I grabbed a few steel dog leashes, holding them up for Liam's approval.

He nodded, looking rather green. I carried them up to the register, figuring the faster Liam got out of this store the better.

Even though Ethan had been teasing Liam about bringing the napkin with him, he did pull them out to pay for the leashes. Ethan had to walk away from the check out counter, he was laughing so hard.

Outside the store, an enormous fountain shaped like a mermaid sat in the center of the square. We crossed the street to sit on the bench next to it.

"So, I was just thinking about something," Ethan said, resting his elbows on his knees and steepling his fingers. "Let's say we pull off the whole plan, we have Aoife in chains and everything. What are we going to do with her when we're done?"

My mouth dropped open. We'd planned the entire thing as far as capturing Aoife, but that's as far as we'd gone. I glanced over at Liam who'd gone from green to ghastly white.

"Well, I don't actually know," he said, blowing out a breath.

"How could we have skipped over this detail?" I said.

"Are you able to run and carry Aoife?" Ethan asked.

Liam nodded. "I am. The steel might slow me down a bit, but I'll still be able to do it."

"Where would he take her?" I asked.

"To Tamhnach? It's just a thought," Ethan said, shrugging.

"It could work. As long as we can hold her long enough," Liam said, a faraway look on his face.

"She'll kill us if we can't," I said.

"We can do this, Al. Don't talk like that," Ethan said, rubbing my knee.

I sighed. "Sorry, you're right. So we bring her back to the castle. Do we leave her there? Do we bring her to Tír na n'Óg?"

"The only way we can end this is if we bring her back to Tír na n'Óg," Liam said.

I tried to think positive, but my fear was stronger than my optimism. "Who's to say it will end if she's brought back there?"

"I don't know," Liam said. "At this point, we just have to have faith that it will all work out."

I didn't like that plan. Relying on faith or hope sounded too much like a fairy tale, one where everyone lived happily ever after and the bad guys were banished, never to be seen again.

"If Aodhan is still in charge or setting things right, he'll make sure she's secure."

As much as I trusted Aodhan, the idea of leaving my family's fate in someone else's hands was unacceptable. I imagined myself face to face with Aoife again, a dagger in my hand. But this time, instead of giving her a surface wound, I imagined plunging it deep into her chest.

"Al?" Ethan said, concerned.

"Hmm?"

"What's going on in that head of yours? You look like you're ready to kill someone," he said.

I straightened my spine and tried to clear my expression. How right he was. "I'm just thinking of how this will go.

"I can't help thinking Saoirse let Aoife out of the fey globe, and what if she just lets her go again? Will she kill my mother? She could come after us all."

"That's not doing you any good, thinking about that right now. Why don't we go for a little walk?" Ethan said.

"We should probably find someplace to hunker down where we won't be seen," Liam said.

He pointed at a large clock across the street from where we sat. "It's quarter after two. We can look around at the gift shop over there for a bit, I suppose."

"I see two things I know Allison would like to do more," Ethan said, grabbing my elbow and turning me. He pointed at one sign that read *Kerrigan's Books*, and another that simply said *The Ice Cream Parlour.*

"I don't see myself having much reading time in the near future, so let's go with the ice cream."

Liam pushed up from the bench and started walking toward the ice cream parlour. Just as quickly, he stopped and spun on his heel, pulling a napkin out of his pocket and grinning. "My treat."

Chapter Fourteen

Not much eased my mind like ice cream. Ethan found us a seat and said he wanted to surprise me. He and Liam got in line, which was unexpectedly long for October. I guessed I wasn't the only one who found solace in hot fudge and whipped cream.

When they returned, Ethan carried a bowl big enough to feed ten. My eyes widened at the unearthly amounts of ice cream and toppings.

He placed the bowl in front of me, and I think I may have sighed in anticipation. "This is a Forbidden Chocolate Lava Sundae," he said with a flourish.

"Wow." It was all I could say. "Where's yours?" I asked when he sat down across from me.

Liam snickered and took a bite from his ice cream cone.

Ethan shook his head and laughed. "I thought you might let me have a bite or two."

I pulled the bowl closer and frowned. "You're kidding, right?"

"I told you to get your own," Liam said, his shoulders shaking with laughter.

Ethan rubbed a hand over his chest. "You wound me."

I shot him a look, trying not to laugh. "Fine, you can have a bite," I said, handing over the extra spoon.

Ethan had made a good call. Eating something delicious and talking about unimportant things definitely made the time go by much faster. When we finished, it was almost time to go. We grabbed our bag of steel leashes and went on the lookout for a cab.

Once Liam pre paid our fare, we climbed into the cab. I turned in my seat to wave to Liam, swallowing the lump of fear in my throat as we pulled away from the curb.

Ethan put his arm across the back of the seat and angled his body toward mine. "Everything's going to be fine," he said in a low voice. "Okay?"

I nodded and tried to put on a brave face. "I just want to be done with it."

It was weird traveling on the left side of the road. Before June of this year, I'd never even left New England. Someday I hoped to come back to Ireland under better circumstances. It was so beautiful and I'd only been able to see a small part.

Ethan must have sensed my need for quiet. We didn't speak much during the drive, but he kept his arm over my shoulders.

Dark clouds moved across the sky, blocking out the sun. A fine mist fell on the windshield, barely enough for the driver to put on his wipers. He had the heat on full blast, since it was so damp and raw. On our way to pick up the cab, Liam had bought the three of us black *Save Tara* hoodies. We looked like ridiculous tourists, but at least we were warm.

We arrived at the entrance to the Hill of Tara just after four o'clock. Ethan and I walked up to the gate where a sign read *Boyne Valley Visitors Center Open for Admission 31 October 17:00- 21:00.*

"The gate is locked," I said, giving it a shake.

"That won't be a problem," Liam said, strolling up to my side. His hair was a little wind-blown, but otherwise you'd never be able to tell he'd just run thirty miles.

"Oh, yeah?" Ethan said. "How's that?"

Liam fixed a steady stare on us. "We'll be glamoured. Rules of admission do not apply."

Ethan grinned. "Even me?"

"Even you."

"Nice," Ethan said, looking down at his arms.

"Follow me," Liam said as he walked around the visitors enter. There was a short fence, but we hopped over it easily.

A few people were scattered over the field stretched out before us. The land was dotted with burial mounds thousands of years old. I'd read a little about Tara and the Hill of Hostages before we came. This place was rich with legends of kings from hundreds and thousands of years ago.

"See that cross?" Liam asked, pointing to a large stone cross surrounded by a low iron fence.

"It marks the spot of the Battle of Tara Hill in the late eighteenth century. On top of that mound behind it is the Stone of Destiny. It was moved to this spot after the battle to honor the soldiers who died."

"The Danaans brought the stone here, right?" I asked.

Liam nodded. "That's what they say. I was brought up believing it was used as a coronation stone for the High Kings. But as it turns out, it was a gift from the Danaans to the High Kings. The properties of the fháillan increased their power, and they didn't even know it."

"Saoirse told me it's the largest piece of fháillan in existence," I said.

"Right," Liam said, squinting at the stone. "Which is why Aoife needs to use it."

"If Aoife were to show up here right now, we'd be screwed," Ethan said.

"Yes. Let's go across to that hedge," Liam said, pointing toward another hill about five hundred yards behind the Stone. "We can keep out of sight over there."

At the bottom of the hedge, pale pink, star-shaped wildflowers still held on to their blooms. We sat on the cold, damp ground, the fragrance from the flowers spreading with the chilly wind.

We stayed quiet. We wouldn't be seen by the locals, but if by any chance Aoife was within earshot, we didn't want to risk her overhearing us.

The clouds scattered, halting the cool, misty rain. As the sun lowered over the horizon, it cast the green hills around us in a glorious golden tone.

Every few minutes one of us peaked over the hedge to see what was going on with the festivities. There was a crew assembling four large, curved metal plates into a fire pit on the flat field between the burial mounds. Liam told me they weren't allowed to light a bonfire directly on the ground.

A crowd of people gathered at the gate as the sky darkened. Men and women carried torches around, adding a sense of ancient mystery to the landscape.

When the gate opened, we stood, the cloak of darkness keeping us hidden. The bonfire was lit by the torchbearers, starting as a tiny flame but quickly igniting into a crackling blaze.

A group of musicians set up not far from where we hid. One held a large frame drum, another a set of pipes and the third a tin whistle like Aodhan's. One of them did a count of three and the night was filled with the sounds of a haunting Irish tune.

A coil of panic seized my chest. I was so scared of what was in store, that my fingers started going numb. But there was no turning back now, this was what we'd been hoping and planning for since I'd first met Liam over the summer. It was bigger than me or the fear spreading through my limbs.

Ethan wrapped his arm around my waist, leaning down to whisper in my ear. "This is going to work," he said.

I leaned my head on his shoulder, hoping a fraction of his confidence might rub off on me. Feeling his arm, firm and strong around my waist kept my fear under control.

Liam watched the bonfire, determined set to his jaw. The flames reflected in the clear blue of his eyes, and I could see that no matter what it cost him, he was ready. Ready to take back his freedom from the one who'd stolen it from him all those years ago. As I watched, it came to me that he was as much a prisoner as my mother.

Liam turned, his eyes searching mine. "Are you ready?" he asked.

I nodded, and Ethan handed me two of the leashes. I stuffed them into the front pocket of my hoodie. He threaded his fingers through mine and we followed Liam out from behind the hedge.

A crisp wind stirred my hair around my face. It was time. Everything we'd been through had led us here. Ethan squeezed my hand, undoubtedly sensing my tension. I looked up and the clouds blew across the star studded sky. The air was thick with the smell of wet grass and burning wood.

Liam slowed, glancing back at us over his shoulder. "No signs of her yet," he whispered.

The hill where the Stone of Destiny sat was empty. We moved through the people circled around the bonfire, getting closer to the base of the hill.

"Stay close," Liam said, tension seeping out of him. "Don't leave the crowd yet."

Nodding, I watched the spot on the hill. My heart was beating as fast as the drum behind us. The moment I heard Liam's sharp intake of breath, I knew Aoife was there.

I licked my lips, trying to see. Squinting and tilting my head away, I saw her form melt out of the darkness. She had her back to us, her hands extended so they rested on the Stone of Destiny. She was wearing tight jeans and a cropped black jacket, her black curls half pulled up on top of her head.

"Can you hear what she's saying?" Liam asked.

"No," I said. "I can't hear anything besides the music and the fire."

He motioned for us to move in closer. "I'm going to

walk around the south side of the hill so she'll see me coming. You two get yourselves just to the bottom until you see me raise my right hand. When I do, you strike."

We nodded and Liam disappeared into the night. Ethan and I edged closer to the hill, away from the crowd.

For several minutes, I couldn't see anything beyond Aoife. But then I could just make out Liam's pale skin and dark sweatshirt as he approached her. A sense of foreboding travelled up my spine as I watched him move in.

He was speaking, but it was too low for me to hear. He looked angry, and I could see the fiery look in his eyes.

"You go for her legs, I'll get her arms," Ethan whispered.

I pulled the chains out of my pocket and wrapped them around my hands. Without tearing his eyes from her, Liam raised his right hand, and Ethan and I took off up the hill running.

When we were just a dozen yards away, I could make out a knife in one of her hands and a cup in the other. Liam said her name and she dropped the cup, which clattered on the stones under her feet.

Liam reached out to knock the knife from Aoife's hand. She grabbed his arm with her other hand just as Ethan and I reached them. Bright light enveloped the hill and when I lunged to wrap the chains around her legs, the ground fell out from under me.

Chapter Fifteen

The light was too intense. I ducked my head into my elbow to keep it from burning my eyes. I tried to make sense of what was happening, but I felt like I was falling blindly into an abyss. Voices were shouting all around me, too muffled and distorted for me to understand.

My knees hit something hard and I fell forward onto my hands. When I raised my head, the light had faded and I was no longer on the Hill of Tara. I blinked and turned my head. Ethan was on his back a few feet from me. To his left, Liam still had his hand wrapped around Aoife's wrist where they lay on their sides.

One minute we were capturing Aoife and the next we were on the floor of a cave.

Aoife staggered to her feet, and Liam shot toward her. She waved a hand and he fell back as though he'd hit a stone wall.

Her eyes darted to where Ethan and I were starting to get to our feet. I met her gaze and our eyes locked.

"You again," she said with a sneer. Her gaze traveled over to Ethan and I felt my pulse spike as her lips formed a wicked smile. "And you brought your friend."

Liam was on his feet again. "Aoife, what is going on?"

She froze and looked to the side. "I guess you met our daughter, hmm Liam?"

"Yes, Aoife. I have met *my* daughter. The one you've

kept from me all this time."

She waved her hand. "Oh, now. It's not uncommon for my kind to foster their children with another family."

"But you never told me about her. How could you do that?"

"Would that have made you want to stay?" she asked, spinning around to face him.

"That's not the point. I had a right to know I had a child."

Aoife's lips curved up. "None of that matters anymore, don't you see?"

I snapped out of my fog of disbelief. "What in the world are you talking about?"

She turned her sinister smile to me. Her eyes were the brightest blue, the color of the azure sky. "You're so quick to trust, aren't you little human girl?"

Liam gritted his teeth and charged forward again only to be thrown back once more.

I tried to run to him, but Ethan pulled me back with a warning look.

"Getting you to come after me was far too easy, really," Aoife said, shaking her head. "Speaking of the binding within Samantha's earshot started the chain of events exactly as my mother predicted. Samantha would go running to find her daddy, you'd come rushing in to save the day, with no idea how implausible the idea of you outsmarting me might be."

A wave of understanding rolled over me. Saoirse let Aoife out of the fey globe. She saw everything, planned every move like we were all life-size chess pieces. But why?

I struggled against the vice grip Ethan had on my arm. I wanted to hurt Aoife. Whether or not I was just a foolish human, I wanted to make her pay for all she'd done to Liam and my mother. And me.

"There's just one little detail that didn't go according to plan," Aoife said, tapping her lip. "You two weren't supposed to make it through." She looked at Ethan and me as if we were a terrible nuisance.

"Through what?" I asked through gritted teeth.

"The veil between our worlds," she said, like she was talking to an idiot. "The binding ceremony needs far more fháillan than just the Stone of Destiny."

"What is this place, Aoife?" Liam said, his hands curled into fists. "Why are we here?"

"This is the last of the fháillan mines," Aoife said, looking around. "The power in this place will allow us to forget about your human attachments. Permanently."

I managed to get out of Ethan's grip and charged toward Aoife. She held her hand up and I just *stopped*. I couldn't move my arms, my legs...I couldn't even blink. Over her shoulder, I saw two figures approaching, but I couldn't make out who they were in the dim cave.

Aoife laughed, dark and melodious. She picked the dagger up off the stone floor and walked toward me. Liam was frozen where he stood, a murderous glint in his eyes.

"No," Ethan said behind me. "Please, no."

Aoife's gaze darted over my shoulder to where Ethan stood, but she continued toward me, holding the dagger out.

One of the figures behind Aoife came into view. *Ciarán.* He held one finger up to his lips and threw out his other hand. Samantha came to his side, eyes wide and panicked.

Aoife pulled back the dagger, just five paces from me. Ciarán brought his hand down and a shower of stalactites from the ceiling of the cave came raining down between me and Aoife.

"Run!" Ciarán shouted, loud enough to be heard over the rocks and rubble cascading to the cave floor.

Aoife fell to her knees and the hold she had on me shattered. I didn't need to be told twice. Spinning around, I searched for a way out of the cave. Liam hollered something, but I couldn't make out what he was saying. Ethan grabbed my elbow and we sprinted toward a tunnel in one of the far corners.

It grew darker as we ran, but we didn't slow down. Adrenaline coursed through my veins and my only thought was to keep moving forward, as far away from Aoife as possible.

The tunnel opened into a narrow passageway that crossed a deep canyon. We skidded to a stop just before we came to the passage.

"We have to make sure it's safe," Ethan said.

"There's no time," I said, glancing back over my shoulder. Liam hadn't come up behind us.

"We'll make time," he said, searching the cave floor. "I just want to throw a rock out there to see if it holds."

He found a rock the size of a basketball and hefted it out onto the passage. The rock broke apart, but the passage held strong.

"Come on," Ethan said, holding out his hand to me.

We moved across the narrow walkway, one tiny step at a time. I kept my eyes trained on Ethan's back. If I looked down, I'd lose my balance and I couldn't see the bottom of the canyon.

"Easy," he whispered and I realized how hard my grip on his hand was.

I swallowed. "Sorry."

"Almost there. Just a few more steps now."

I placed one foot in front of the other until we got to the small landing on the other side.

I crumpled in relief once we made it. Ethan wrapped his arms around me, keeping me upright.

"We aren't safe yet," he said into my neck. "We have to keep going."

Footsteps from across the passageway stopped us. I turned to see Liam come to a halt outside the tunnel.

"It's safe," Ethan called over.

Liam nodded and started running across when the walls over his head came crumbling down. He was propelled forward, hanging by one hand to the stone passageway.

"Liam," I said, starting toward him. Once again, Ethan's hands gripped my arm, holding me in place. "What are you doing? We have to help him."

He nodded toward the avalanche spreading down to the passageway. A fissure cracked straight through the center and Liam's eyes widened in panic.

I screamed in horror as the stone gave way under his fingers, plunging him into the depths of the canyon below.

Liam would catch something to break his fall. He had to. Because no one could survive a fall like that. No amount of magic could undo those injuries.

I looked back at Ethan and the expression in his eyes shattered my heart into a thousand pieces. "No. No, no, no," I said.

He swallowed, and the pity I saw in his expression undid me. "We have to go back, he'll make it."

"We need to get out of here, Al. You know that. Come on," he said, holding out a hand for me.

I ignored it, but started moving forward. Away from the still crumbling passage. My whole body was going numb. If I could just get out of this cave, I could collapse and just let my emotions pull me under.

The sounds of destruction grew louder and we ran faster. The ground was quaking and shifting under our feet. I didn't know what direction we were heading, but I just kept pushing forward blindly.

"Up there," Ethan said, pointing to a spot of light at the end of the tunnel, high above the ground. Rocks were piled on top of one another, forming a hill.

We started climbing up, but the rocks were unstable and we slid down faster than we could climb. My foot caught on a wobbly stone, sending me tumbling back toward the cave. The rocks sliced into my skin where I crashed into them, until I finally rolled to a stop, landing so that my ankle was bent backward. Pain flared up my leg and I cried out. Ethan came sliding down the rocks until he was at my side.

His eyes scanned over my body, taking in my injuries. He froze when he saw how I held my ankle. "Is it broken?" he asked.

I sucked in a harsh breath. "I'm not sure. But we have to keep going."

"Hold on to me," he said and I grabbed his bicep as he helped me to my knees. The pain spasmed through me when I tried to put pressure on my right foot. I climbed on, favoring my left side while Ethan helped pull me up.

Once we made it to the top of the hill, I could see the blue sky of Tír na n'Óg through the opening. We climbed out, Ethan half carrying me, and stopped on the ridge to rest.

He pulled off my shoe and sock to examine my ankle, and let out a string of curses. I looked down. My foot had already turned a sickening blackish blue all the way to my pinky toe and was grotesquely swollen.

I closed my eyes and called out to Samantha in my mind. She didn't answer. I just sat there, cold and stunned.

Ethan moved up to sit by my side and wrapped an arm around my shoulders. I buried my face into his side, breathing in his familiar scent and letting it surround me.

"I don't know what to do," he whispered into my hair.

I shook my head and sighed. "It was all a sham. Saoirse knew what Aoife was up to. She even helped her. How could I have been so stupid?"

Ethan's hand tightened on my shoulder. "You weren't stupid. They had us both fooled."

"I wonder if they all knew, even Niamh. And were all laughing at the stupid humans trying to go up against their kind."

"It doesn't matter," he said, kissing my head.

"My mother," I said with a sob. "If Liam's gone, what's going to happen to my mother?"

He shook his head. "I'm sorry, Al. I just don't know."

I sucked in a sharp breath and pulled back, searching his

eyes. Tears built in mine and I squeezed them shut. "Oh God. She'll die of a broken heart. I'll lose them both," I said, a sob tearing through me.

"Shh," he said, pulling my head down and cradling me to his chest.

Once I'd cried myself out, I lifted my head and sniffed. "We need to get away from here," I said, wiping tears away.

Below the cave's entrance, the gravel made way to a grassy hill. Ethan stood and helped me up. He draped my right arm over his shoulder and supported my weight as we walked down, away from the cave.

Two figures appeared in front of us. They moved so fast, all I could see was a blur. I was lifted off my good foot and when I blinked I was looking up into Aodhan's concerned face.

"What's happened?" he asked, eyes wide.

I turned my head and Ethan was staring at where I had been just a second ago. Niamh came to a stop beside where Aodhan held me in a cradle hold.

"How are you here?" I said to Niamh.

"My mother came and told us about a vision she'd had. She said we needed to come right away," Niamh said and looked back up to Aodhan.

"Saoirse had you come to help us?" I asked. "That makes no sense."

Niamh nodded. "She said Aoife had changed her plan at the last minute and you were in danger. Where is she? Where's Liam?"

"There's a fháillan mine deep within that cave," I said, pointing back the way we'd come. "She was about to kill me and Ethan and do the binding, but Ciarán showed up and stopped her. He caused a rockslide and we just barely made it out. Liam...Liam didn't make it."

"Come, let's get you back to my house," Niamh said, her face pinched. "It's not far from here."

"Wait, what if Liam somehow makes it out?" I said,

seeing Aoife in my mind somehow rescuing him and continuing with the binding.

Aodhan's jaw hardened. Niamh looked away.

"Liam knows his way, right?" Ethan said, glancing between them.

"Of course," Niamh said, but she didn't meet my eyes.

Aodhan carried me to Niamh's house and Ethan stayed by my side as he walked. When we arrived, Aodhan sat me in one of the chairs in Niamh's dining room. I laid my head on the table. My lids felt way too heavy and my thoughts were hazy. It wasn't until then that I realized how much I hurt, inside and out.

The last thing I remember was Ethan standing in front of me. "Is she going to be okay?" he asked, but everything slipped away before I heard the answer.

I opened my eyes to darkness. It took a few minutes before everything that happened came back to me.

I bolted upright and realized I was in a bed. The blankets moved and I felt Ethan sitting up next to me.

"Hey," he said, reaching out a hand and touching my cheek.

"Where are we?" I asked.

"We're in one of Niamh's guest rooms. You were in shock and Eithne said your body needed to shut down so you could rest. You've been sleeping for a few hours."

"Eithne was here? But what about…" Ethan put his finger over my lips

"Shh," he said. "Niamh went to get her after you passed out. She healed your ankle. You had a very nasty break."

I tried moving my foot. There was no pain.

Liam's look of panic flashed in my memory. "Liam. Oh God, Liam."

"Come here," Ethan said, pulling me into his lap and smoothing his hand over my hair.

Tears welled in my eyes and spilled down my cheeks again. I buried my face into Ethan's shoulder. Liam was gone. I'd barely had a chance to know him before he was so violently torn from my life. And chances were my mother would be, too.

"Look at me," Ethan said, grasping my chin to tilt my head up so I'd meet his eyes.

I shook my head. "It's my fault. What was I thinking?"

"You were trying to make things right," he said, wiping away my tears.

I dragged in a ragged breath and nodded. "I was."

"You should try to get some more rest," he said, tilting his head to the side. "And then I want to take you home."

I didn't want to rest, but I did want to go home. As far away from Tír na n'Óg as I could get. Ethan helped me to my feet. For the most part I felt fine, if a tiny bit stiff.

We walked into the dining room where Niamh and Aodhan sat talking with Eithne and Diarmuid. They all looked up when we came in.

Eithne came over to where I sat down and, hands fluttering around me, asked how I was feeling.

"I feel completely fine," I said, my voice still a little wobbly with tears. I sniffed. "I really just want to go home."

"Of course," Niamh said, giving me a tight smile. "We'll go right away."

"I'm coming, too," Aodhan said, getting to his feet.

"But, what about…" Niamh started to say.

"I don't give a damn about any of that," Aodhan said. "Deaghlan can handle that without me."

"Don't leave on my account," I said, frowning at Aodhan.

"I'm coming," he said, and his tone was final.

The journey back was fast and uneventful. I was barely even aware of my surroundings as we went through the portal. Ethan drove us from Wheelwright back to Stoneville and all I could think about was going to my mother. If she were going to be taken from me, too, I wanted to be with her for as long as I could.

We went to Liam's house first so Niamh could call the decoys back and get briefed on what we'd missed.

My decoy said I'd been granted the leave of absence I'd applied for. I'd been working at the hardware store and spending most of my time with Ethan, Jeff and Nicole planning the wedding. Nothing out of the ordinary happened with my mother during our time away. My grandfather had been to a specialist because of chest pains, but they'd put him on medication and he was doing well.

Aodhan didn't say much while the decoys, who'd taken back their own appearances, filled us in. He was just a silent presence in the corner, watching and listening.

Ethan walked me home and stopped at the bottom of my porch steps. "You're awful quiet," he said, giving me a tired smile.

I nodded. "I know, and I'm sorry. I've just been trying to keep control of my thoughts."

His eyebrows knitted. "What do you mean?"

I smoothed my T-shirt. "I didn't want Niamh to know what I'm thinking, so I've been trying to think about things like sunshine and flowers."

"And what are you really thinking about?" he said.

I stood up straight and met his gaze. "I think I'm going to kill Aoife, or die trying."

Acknowledgments

A great big thank you to my family for putting up with me when I go for days without coming out of my book-writing fog. To my husband Kevin and four kiddos— I love you even if I ignore you!

A special shout-out to my Super Sekrit Ninjas for their undying support through the last year. I love that I can always count on you!

I'm so grateful for the book community we have on FB— authors, bloggers, editors, etc. Thank you for putting up with all my random questions and rants!

And thank you last, but not least to my editor Becky Tsaros Dickson for helping me to write more and write better.

About the Author

Laura Howard lives in New Hampshire with her husband and four children. Her obsession with books began at the age of 6 when she got her first library card. Nancy Drew, Sweet Valley High and other girly novels were routinely devoured in single sittings. Books took a backseat to diapers when she had her first child. It wasn't until the release of a little novel called Twilight, 8 years later, that she rediscovered her love of fiction. Soon after, her own characters began to make themselves known.

Blog:
http://laurahoward78.blogspot.com/

Twitter:
https://twitter.com/LauraHoward78

Facebook:
https://www.facebook.com/LauraHoward78